Nine Minutes and Counting

Jennifer Ann McGee

"One of the most difficult things to think about in life is one's regrets. Something will happen to you, and you will do the wrong thing and for years afterward you will wish you had done something different."

-Lemony Snickett, Horseradish

This book is lovingly dedicated to the one I carry with me,
always in my heart,
CJ.

Prologue:

The night was always the hardest.

I would count myself to sleep, but once asleep, my dreams were out of my grasp. My dreams brought me to places I didn't want to be.

Night after night, Connor would enter my dreams like a movie star taking center stage. It was then that I could hear his voice, "See me Sissy, see me." That was always what he said when he wanted to be picked up. "See me, see me," his little hands raised in the air beckoning me to bring him into the fold of my arms.

I would bend to pick him up, and the vicious night Gods would intercept.

I could never get my hands on him. I could never quite get to him. Just when he would be inches from my reach, I would wake up and realize I was just dreaming. Again.

Most nights JoJo slept next to me. Maybe Connor made his way to her in her dreams too. I never knew. We didn't talk about it. But many, many nights after I awakened from my dreams, I sobbed silently into my pillow, drenching my pillowcase with angry streams of disappointment-soaked tears.

One night, like so many other nights, I fell into a fitful sleep. In my dream, I found myself back at Beaver Brook Campground. I could smell the fresh balsam of the pine needles. I could see the tree house through the boughs. There at the end of the path, I could see Connor.

It was so good to see him. He was playing cheerfully near the swings, holding Duffy in his hand. I could make out the spoked B on his backwards Red Sox baseball cap. I started to run toward him.

"Connor, Connor, wait right there," I yelled through the trees. "Connor, it's me. Lizzie. Wait," and I sprinted in his direction as fast as I could.

Connor started heading away from the swings, toddling in his little alligator crocs toward the woods. No, no, no. Wait there. Wait for me.

I tried to catch up. He was so little, but I couldn't catch him.

Branches were slapping my face, twigs slicing into my shins. "Connor," I heard myself scream. "Connor, stop."

As I ran deeper into the woods, thick brush and thorny branches continued to dig and claw at my legs. The needle-sharp spines of the pine bristles poked me in the face as I pushed through trying to find my baby brother.

"Connor buddy, Connor, answer me," I was crying now. "Connor, please, " and breathless I kept running. Where was he? How did he get away from me? My lungs burned as I ran and ran.

Finally, I spotted a clearing straight ahead. There was a little patch where dappled light shone through. I ran for the light. I broke through the forest, and there in the clearing stood

Connor. I could see him reaching for a stone in the swiftly moving, inches deep brook in front of him. There, just ahead of him was a shiny granite river stone that would fit perfectly in his little palm.

He was right there. Just in front of me. I lunged in his direction, and grabbed him by the back of his shirt. I plucked him up and buried my head in the nape of his neck, relieved to have him in my arms. He startled and turned to look at me. He gave me a big toothy smile, "Sissy," he said in his raspy two year old voice. "Sissy," and he proudly held up the shiny, wet stone for me to see.

I woke up.

Nooooooooo, no, no, no…

The nights were so cruel.

Chapter 1:

One of the earliest memories I have is when I was three, maybe four, years old. I was standing in the window of the screen door of our kitchen. The rain outside was falling in sheets and I was pressing my hands over my ears in terror. Tears were squeezing out of the corner of my eyes, my lips quivering. Thunderous booms were exploding from the sky. The sonic quakes shook the floor where I stood.

"Lizzie," Daddy said, scooping me up easily into the crook of his big, muscular truck-driving arms. "Don't be afraid. It's just a little ole thunder. It won't hurt you."

"But it's s-s-so l-l-loud," I barely got out with my face pressed into his shoulder.

"Lizzie, it's not the thunder you have to worry about. That's just a little noise. It's the lightning you have to watch out for. The lightning is the dangerous part of any storm."

Another clap of thunder forced me to bury my head deep into my father's neck. His neck smelled of safety. He held me tight. "Lizzie," his gentle voice calmed me, "I am going to teach you a trick that your granddaddy taught me when I was a little knee biter."

I leaned back to listen. "If you want to find out how far away the storm is, you can count. As soon as you see the lightning, start counting, and stop counting when you hear the clap of the thunder. Let's try it."

With my eyes squeezed shut, I braced myself for the next giant clap of thunder with my hands pressed over my ears and my body clenched in fear. But instead of thunder, there it was...a jagged blinding bolt of lightning filling the sky. Together, we began counting.

"One, one thousand, two, one thousand, three, one thousand, four, one thousand, five, one thousand, six, one thousand, seven, one thousand, eight...." KA-KA-KA POW, an enormous booming thunderclap erupted.

"That's it," Daddy said. "The storm is eight miles away."

Life is filled with storms. What I didn't know then was that most of life's storms have nothing to do with thunder and lightning.

Chapter 2:

It's funny how things have been one way for a very long time, and then suddenly they are very different. But pretty soon, you can hardly remember the way things used to be.

It's like when you have a really sore throat.   All you can think about is how it feels like razor blades are scoring the sides of your throat when you try to swallow. You can't even remember how it used to feel in your throat when you were healthy and well and eating corn chips. You can only feel the pain that is happening right then and there.

That's how it was for me. There was my life BBB (Before Beaver Brook) and my life ABB (After Beaver Brook).

Before Beaver Brook, I had a mother who stayed home with me and Connor and JoJo. She got up in the morning before we got up and she got us up ready for school. I didn't really even pay much attention to it. It's just the way it always was.

She would come into our bedrooms in the morning and put her face just in front of ours. I could smell her minty mouthwash and her freshly shampooed hair. "Good morning my beautiful princesses," she would say.

When JoJo and I grumpily opened our eyes, there she was. She was leaning over us, dressed and pony-tailed, with a genuine smile as if we truly were royal princesses she was so happy to find asleep in the beds we were always in.

We would stretch and yawn, and she would quickly reach into our bureau drawers and pull from our closets our school clothes for the day. When we were getting dressed, she would be behind us, sometimes with Connor toddling along beside her, fluffing our pillows, tightly tucking in our bed sheets and pulling our pink comforters up, perfectly making our beds. She would pull up our blinds and yank open our lacy curtains to let the daylight stream in.

While we went to the bathroom, she would have our breakfast all set out on the table. She would cut up fresh melons or sprinkle apple slices with cinnamon. Our breakfast cereal would be prepared with almond milk poured, and toast with butter and strawberry jam. Mondays were special, she would say, "to get the week started right," and she would have a hot breakfast: French toast, or pancakes or scrambled eggs with sprinkles of cheese.

On the counter sat two lunch boxes: mine and JoJo's. The contents were pretty much the same each day: a sandwich, tuna for JoJo, ham and cheese for me, a fruit, a tiny bag of something crunchy (chips, or goldfish, or pretzels) and a thermos of ice water. I never knew anything different. Some days Mom would pop a note into our lunches. It might say: **Make today a great one**, or: **I am so proud of you**, or: **I love you princess**. She always signed our notes like this: **xoxoxo, M**

That was just how it was, forever… or so I thought.

Flash forward to now, ABB (After Beaver Brook).

At first, I used to be hopeful that Mom would be out in the kitchen when we rounded the corner to use the bathroom, but that never happened. She wouldn't be in the kitchen. She would be in bed…where she spends most of her time.

Every morning I rummage through my closet to find something decent to wear. Middle school fashion is important. Really important. I try to find the same things everyone at school is wearing. I find jeans from the Gap or Old Navy, or something. Dad let me order a Vineyard Vines sweatshirt online so I wear that a lot. I already feel like a freak at school, so I don't want my clothes to make me look like a bigger freak than I already am.

JoJo is another story. She is a tomboy through and through, so even though Mom had taken her to get some decent "girlie" clothes, now that I am "in charge" she won't wear any of it.

Every day she battles me, wearing the same boy clothes: camouflage pants and shirts, day after day. Finally I have given up. She is a tyrant about her clothes, so she heads to school each day looking like a hot mess, nine year old little boy/girl. I surrender.

I fix her hair in barrettes or a ponytail...whatever is quick and easy. She doesn't give me too much hassle about her hair because she can't stand to have her hair in her face. Most likely she's too busy out at recess playing chase to want to mess with her hair. Mom would be pleased with JoJo's hair. She would not be pleased with what JoJo is wearing.

Breakfast is also whatever is quick and easy. Dad got us Pop Tarts, Bagel Bites (which I tried to explain to JoJo isn't breakfast food....but then I tried it...and I thought, why not), Toaster Strudels. Then I make the lunches. I tried to get into a routine of doing it the night before, but I just got busy with homework, and I couldn't make myself prepare lunches ahead of time. Now I just do it in a hurry before 7:30. JoJo hates my lunches, but tuna is too much work. I told her, "Tuna was BBB (Before Beaver Brook), now it's ham and cheese."

Right before we leave, we peek into Mommy's room. I bring her some juice and whatever we had for breakfast, and I place it on her nightstand. She has the shades down. Her room is dark except for the blue light of her digital clock. She rolls over when we come into the room, and looks at us. We both stand by the edge of the bed.

"Bye Mommy. Have a good day," JoJo says.

"Do you need anything Mom?" I always ask.

"Just be good girls," Mom always says. "I love you."

"We love you too Mommy," we say as we bend to kiss her.

She always ends our morning visit with, "I'm sorry girls. I am so sorry," and her voice breaks.

We always tell her it's okay. But it isn't.

Chapter 3:

Dad was driving. Mom sat in the passenger seat next to him with a Starbucks Coffee in her hand. Her paper cup always had the same half moon of Mom's tinted lip gloss on the edge. The three of us sat behind our parents, nearly jumping out of our skin with excitement at the adventure just ahead.

JoJo, my eight, almost nine, year old sister, sat in the backseat of the Jeep Cherokee with Connor, our two year old little, blonde, blue-eyed, most of the time snotty-faced, brother, strapped into his car seat between us. Connor's constant companion, his stuffed elephant was clutched in his dimpled fist. First on one side, then the other, he took turns pretending to drop it. "Oopsy," he would say in between fits of giggles.

"Oh no Connor," JoJo and I would tease, "You dropped Duff. Where can it be?" First me, then JoJo, entertaining our two-year-old brother for the three hour car ride to Beaver Brook. The game never got old for Connor. It got very old for JoJo and me.

"Oopsy," Mom and Dad could hear from the backseat, and they exchanged silent smiles with one another. Dad laid his hand over Mom's, and they rode like this for several minutes as the radio played country music, Clint Black's voice filling the Jeep: *"When I said that I do, I meant that I will...til the end of all time, be faithful and devoted to you..."* Daddy sang along with every word as he always does. Mommy smiled and tapped her fingers to the music. She never sang along, because she loved listening to Daddy sing. Plus, she said she "couldn't carry a tune in a tub". As she tapped along to the music, Daddy put his hand over hers.

I reached down for Duff, again and again, noticing Mom and Dad holding hands. For some reason it made me embarrassed whenever Mom and Dad were affectionate, like I was witnessing something I wasn't supposed to be seeing. I just knew, this was going to be the best weekend ever.

As long as I could remember, we had been going to Beaver Brook Campground for Labor Day weekend. It was always our last "hurrah" of summer...almost making me forget that school would be starting the day after we got back.

The back of the Jeep held our "provisions". Our enormous family tent was the first thing tossed into the hatch. Jo and I loved tenting because Dad would let us sleep together in the zip up screen porch of our tent. It made us feel so grown up and independent with Mom, Dad and Connor in the main part of the tent, and JoJo and I outside in the screen room. I was praying we could do that again.

Coolers, air mattresses, life jackets, reusable grocery bags filled with the required food for camping: Pringles, Dinty Moore Beef Stew, baked beans, juice boxes, Jiffy Pop Popcorn...the usual. We had mounds of duffel bags with clothes, bathing suits and beach towels. Dad had to use his side mirrors because he couldn't see out the back window the back was so heaped with stuff!

We could hardly stand the excitement of arriving at our beloved campsite. Sis and I were on pins and needles waiting to round the familiar corner of Beaver Brook. The decades old, hand painted wooden signs greeted us...*We welcome you to*....and ¼ mile later...*Beaver Brook*...and then after another ¼ mile...*We're mighty glad you're here!* And then another ¼ mile through the grove of stately pine trees...a picture of the famous Beaver standing next to the brook with a fishing pole in his hand was the final sign.

We were finally at Beaver Brook! Together, JoJo and I began the countdown of campsites. Mom and Dad exchanged knowing smiles as the tradition began. "There's site number 1!"....a bit farther down the lane...."site number 5"....farther on..."Yayyyyyy...site number 7!! We're here!"

Daddy stretched behind the steering wheel, after the long drive, and said the same thing he always said as he turned around to look at the three of us with a giant grin, "Lucky number 7. Let's get this party started campers!"

Chapter 4:

Camp Site # 7 was ours! Every year we asked for campsite 7. It was sandwiched in between the lakefront beach and the forest play yard! There was plenty of room to set up our giant tent and there was a nice smooth spot to unroll our sleeping bags for a good night's sleep. Every year, as soon as we got back home, we would make our next year's reservation for Lucky #7.

JoJo and I could hardly stand the time it took to unpack. It was too much to wait before heading to the playground to search for our old friends, but Mom and Dad were strict about being good helpers while we were camping. Dad always said, "Camping is a team sport."

Mom was quick to remind us, "Girls, camping is where I learned all of my survival skills. I learned how to fend for myself by camping with my parents, and I want you to learn the same things!"

JoJo and I rolled our eyes behind her back. I was thinking, "Hmmmm..." I wasn't exactly sure what Mom meant by 'fending' for herself, but she wasn't exactly my top pick for Survivor. She is a pretty good cook, but I couldn't picture her starting up our camp fire or hunting food for our dinner. Not without Dad. She never even put a worm on a fishing hook, but whatever, we pitched in.

One heavy item by one heavier item, JoJo and I begrudgingly helped unpack the Jeep.

The first order of business was always unloading all of the gear, and as we unpacked the Jeep, Mom and Dad erected our giant tent. They should sell "old tent smell" like "new car smell". The fragrance of damp canvas, with woodsy pine, and a hint of dirt delivered years of Beaver Brook camping memories: campfires, s'mores, starry nights, ghost stories, damp and rainy camping days filled with card games and cribbage. Luckily, Mom and Dad had a system and were experienced at setting up the tent.

Dad took charge. He told Mom where to place the stakes, and then came around with a hammer to get the edges tethered. Like a well-oiled machine, Dad barked out orders, and Mom followed them. They had it up in record time! They stood back and bumped fists.

Dad inflated the air mattresses and just as I hoped, he popped two air mattresses out onto the screen porch for JoJo and me. We would get to sleep in the screen porch after all! "Hey girls, looks like your hotel accommodations are ready. Will this be suitable for your highnesses?" Dad asked grinning, knowing how much we both really wanted to sleep on the screen porch!

Mom added a few homey touches to our campsite every year, while Dad just rolled his eyes. This year she proudly set a big pot of golden marigolds outside of the screen porch and a large indoor/outdoor green carpet with the word: WELCOME.

JoJo and I ran to get our LLBean sleeping bags unrolled and placed on top of our air mattresses. Mine, as the oldest, was placed closest to the zippered door, and JoJo had hers nearest the zipper where Mom and Dad were. Connor toddled along, "oopsy" went Duff the elephant over and over again, but by this time, both JoJo and I had lost interest in that game.

We couldn't wait to make up our beds and head over to the playground to see if our favorite friends, twin sisters from Rhode Island, were back for Labor Day Weekend. Mom scooped Connor up in her arms. "Last year, when we were here, you weren't walking little buddy," Mom said as she kissed the top of his baseball cap. "You are going to be a handful on this trip!"

Connor chortled and then squirmed to get back down and explore the campsite.

Chapter 5:

Mom put Connor down, and hollered, "Girls, Dad and I are going to start the fire and get the food ready for dinner. Keep an eye on Connor while we prepare the meal."

Maybe the best part of camping is the food. "Everything tastes better when it's cooked on an open fire," Dad said to no one in particular as he hunched over the fire pit tearing up strips of newspaper.

I had just turned eleven and JoJo's ninth birthday was coming up. We had just ridden in the Jeep for three hours, playing the annoying "oopsy game" with Connor the entire time. Now that we had arrived at our campsite, we were STILL watching Connor when all we wanted to do was be alone in the tree house.

The playground next to the campsite was magical and it was all we could think about. There was a tree house built on stumps six feet in the air. You had to climb a ladder built of twigs in order to get inside. There were wonderful tire swings hanging from tall oak limbs, and there was an obstacle course designed out of ropes tied into life-sized spider webs and stumps and twisted roots. Last year, they had added a zip line that ran from one giant tall pine to another. It was incredible. Neither one of us wanted to slow down and watch Connor, but we knew this was just part of being big sisters.

Connor toddled his way toward us, his Blues Clues sippy cup was clamped between his front teeth and he was still clutching Duff the ever-present elephant. Connor liked to wear his red Boston Red Sox baseball cap, with its blue "spoked-B", backward on his head. Mom smiled down at her tough little boy with his dusty knees and dirty face. "He would sleep in that cap if I let him," she said absently, patting his diapered bum as he strutted past.

"Mom, can we bring Connor to the playground with us?" JoJo asked hopefully trying to negotiate a compromise.

"He's too little and too busy. Watch him right here girls."

I insisted urgently, "Please Mom. I think he will be able to go on the lower tire swings. He will love the play yard. We will watch him every minute. We're old enough."

Mom and Dad exchanged looks, and Dad nodded. "They will be okay Rosie. They are responsible." And then Dad looked toward the three of us and made an executive decision (which he rarely did without Mom's approval), "Go ahead girls. Just keep an eye on the little guy!"

JoJo and I squealed in delight. Mom cast a wary look in our direction. At the last second, Connor dropped, but then grabbed Duff, stuffing him into his shirt, and off we scrambled toward the playground, hand in hand. Connor was in the middle of his two sisters, swinging happily along the pine needle path.

Chapter 6: Beaver Tree House

It wasn't long before I realized I had been wrong about Connor being big enough for the playground.

When we arrived at the playground, we immediately spotted our camping friends from Rhoda Island. "Hello," called Ruby and Rosie, twin ten year old girls from site # 4, "You came back!"

Yessssss! I was so happy to see them. The weekend was going just as planned, except for having to watch Connor this time.

JoJo and I ran toward them, dragging Connor along. "We were hoping you would be here. Now remind us which is which!" I smiled toward the two of them with my head bobbing inquisitively back and forth from one red- headed, freckled face to the other.

The girl wearing the red Beaver Brook Camping t-shirt quickly came to the rescue, "Remember, I'm Ruby, and this is my sister Rose, pointing next to her mirror image in a blue Beaver Brook t-shirt, "Rose, like your Mom's name."

"Of course we remember you. How could we forget?" I told them laughing. "We were hoping you would be here!"

As we all got caught up and became reacquainted with one another, Connor tugged and tugged and pulled at my hand to go to the tire swings. Exasperated with the tussling toddler, JoJo and the twins and I headed toward the swings, but we all were looking longingly toward the Beaver Tree House on the four stump posts. It was there, last year, that the four of us spent most of our time.

As, JoJo sat on the tire swing, she attempted to hold Connor on her lap. She had to hold onto both the chains of the swing and his little body. Both of them kept slipping and sliding off. No matter how JoJo positioned herself, she could not handle both the swing and Connor. She was growing more and more frustrated and so was he.

I then tried, unsuccessfully, to put Connor on the swing by himself, but his little arms could not reach both chains, and he kept slipping through the middle of the tire. Then we all decided to try crisscrossing our legs to create a basket of legs to put Connor on top of, but he didn't feel secure doing that either. Nothing was working.

I knew everyone wanted to go to the tree house, but the twins were being good sports, trying to figure out how to include Connor. "Let's try the obstacle course," suggested Ruby. We all attempted to coerce Connor toward the obstacle course, but he refused.

"No! Swing! No, no, no…", Connor cried as he plunked himself down on the forest floor of the playground. Nothing would entice him to move. We all tried and tried to get him to follow us. "No, no, swing," he demanded throwing one of his classic, spoiled brat fits.

I rolled my eyes and desperately looked toward the other girls as they abandoned the idea of going to the obstacle course and headed, without me, to the Beaver Tree House. JoJo hollered back to me, "Lizzie, just stay with Connor and meet us when you can get him to move!"

I stayed back with Connor, and over and over again I tried to find a way to make the swing work for him. He slipped and slid, and fell and flopped and refused to move anywhere else in spite of his lack of success. I kept looking across the playground at my sister and our camping friends we had waited all year to see. They were climbing in and out of our favorite spot: The Beaver Tree House! Ugh...Connor was such a pain.

"Thanks for ruining my fun Connor," I said looking down at him.

He scowled, looking up at me, pointing his little index finger, "NO, SWING!" All I could do to keep from shouting at him was to sigh.

Chapter 7:

Dad and Mom had the table all set for dinner. Dad had his "famous" burgers sizzling in the hot cast iron skillet. Mom had plates and silverware at five places on the red -checkered tablecloth. There was a special spot at the end of the table for Connor's booster seat to hang. His placemat was edged in plastic, decorated with dinosaurs and his toddler bowl and spoon sat ready for his favorite dinner of spaghetti-o's and fresh sliced peaches.

Mom placed a large bowl of rotini pasta salad in the center of the table, and she positioned a plate with crisp, freshly sliced cucumbers next to each setting with a dollop of ranch dressing to use for dipping. Hamburger rolls were open and each ready to receive a juicy burger. Ketchup, mustard and relish were standing like soldiers prepared for dinner action!

She also had our favorite camping dessert prepared...dirt cake!!! We all loved the chocolate cake and pudding and whipped cream with gummy worms, in cups like little mounds of delicious mud. Mom could not wait to surprise us after we finished our supper. It would be Connor's first taste of dirt cake and Mom was sure he would love the rubbery yellow, red, and green gummy worms.

"Jon, go get the children for dinner! It's all ready. I will watch the burgers in the skillet to make sure they don't burn."

"Okay, Rosie, my queen. As you wish," and he bowed, kidding around as always, and headed toward the pine needle trail to the playground.

As Dad headed down the trail, Mom thought back to her days as a young girl at Beaver Brook. The sounds and smells and sights were so familiar. She blinked back the tears that came in an instant when she thought about her parents, who she missed so much. They would be so proud of her...with her three children...camping just like they did. They were good tears. Happy tears. She breathed in deeply the scents of the fire, forest, and tent. If she closed her eyes, she could place herself back into her childhood, twenty years ago.

Opening her eyes, she turned back to her perfect table, and waited for us to fill our seats.

Chapter 8:

It was hard to watch the girls all having fun in the Beaver Tree House. I looked longingly at the tiny log cabin up on stilts with its "crookedy" twig ladder. The outside of the tree house was so cute. It had sweet little window boxes with pink and red shade flowers in full bloom. I had waited all summer long to get a chance to play in that special spot. I was feeling so impatient with the squirming and frustrated little toddler at my feet. He was driving me nuts.

Last year, when we climbed into the tree house, it became our "club house". It was really fun to make up special rules for membership. These were our rules:

#1: You must be a girl

#2: You must keep all secrets inside of the tree house

#3: You must be invited before you can come inside

#4: You must always bring something to share before entering

The inside of the tree house was really neat. There were little cushioned benches and the walls were painted in bright primitive colors with a little kitchen and living room. We had fashioned a rope to pull all sorts of wonderful things up into the clubhouse for our meetings. We brought in pillows and snacks and ghost story books to read with flashlights. We all made journals in Beaver Brook Craft Class, and brought those into the clubhouse to keep diaries. It was so much fun. But I was stuck with Connor to contend with, and was missing all of the fun.

"Come on Lizzie," the girls called out of the windows. I just smiled weakly and waved back.

"Come on Connor," I encouraged. "Let's go to the big tree house," I said in my most excited and enthusiastic, sugary sweet voice. "Come on...it will be fun!"

Connor had been pretending Duff the elephant was a car. He had given up on the swing, and instead was running Duff through a little mound of pine needles, over and over again....repeat, repeat, repeat. It never got old for him.

"Brrrrrrrrrmmmmmm," Connor would say. "Car sissy. Duff car." He tossed his head back and laughed and laughed thinking how funny it was that Duff the elephant was now his car. Duff was covered with a fine dust and pine needles were stuck to the long gray trunk. Boring. Boring. Toddlers are so boring.

Over and over again, Connor kept playing the same redundant game. I just sat on the tire swing, dragging my feet through the pine needles, back and forth, back and forth, over and over again, watching Connor play with his revoltingly filthy stuffed elephant. All the while, I could hear the backdrop of sounds coming from the Beaver Tree House. JoJo and Ruby and Rose were laughing, getting caught up, making plans, carefree and happy... in the clubhouse...without yours truly.

I looked down at Connor. He was so content. So happy. He was perfectly entertained playing with Duff in the pine needles. If I brought him to the tree house, I knew he would totally freak out. I would just go. Just go and peek in for *one minute* while Connor played happily with Duff.

I would only be a minute.

Chapter 9:

When I got to the ladder of the tree house, I quickly glanced back at Connor. He was still playing in the needles running Duff through them, back and forth, back and forth. Same old song and dance. He was fine.

I got to the tip-top of the ladder and peeked inside of the clubhouse. It was exactly the same as I had remembered.

The girls were all happy to see me. We started planning all of the adventures we would create in the next three days. I glanced out of the tiny tree house window one more time toward Connor, still playing in the dirt, and so I jumped inside to join in on the planning...just for a minute. I looked down at the white Timex watch my grandmother had given me, on my wrist. It read 5:14. I would be one minute. Then I would head right back to watch Connor.

Ruby had a notebook and she was writing down what we would need for "supplies" for our weekend in the Beaver Tree House. Ruby wrote quickly as we shouted out our lengthy list. We would need Pop Tarts (all of our favorite camping snack), water bottles, we would need UNO cards and board games, comic books, ghost stories, flashlights....

Chapter 10:

"Go get the kids Jon."

"Dinner is ready," Mom had called out to Dad. Mom stood back and admired the red-checkered tablecloth covering the picnic table. She had placed a pot of red geraniums in the center of the table. Five plates, four cups, five sets of silverware were around the table. At the end of the table sat Connor's booster seat with his sippy cup filled with ice cold milk.

Dad whistled absently on his way to the playground. He loved this weekend. Not only did he get to take his beautiful family camping, but Mom was always so happy on this weekend. Since she had lost her parents, she hadn't been the same. She was always more quiet, more nervous, more...well, just kind of sad.

Mom had been a lot better the past few months, but there were times when Dad could see how sad she was, and how hard she was trying. Trying to enjoy life. Trying to enjoy us, all of us.

Camping at Beaver Brook seemed to bring Mom back to us.

When Mom's parents, Grammy and Grampy, died in a car accident, it was like they had taken a part of Mom with them. Somehow, at Beaver Brook, she seemed like herself again.

Grammy and Grampy used to always bring Mom to Beaver Brook when she was a kid. When she was here, I think she remembered those times. I could see a far away look in her eye...like she was remembering...like she was seeing herself as a child. And she would smile.

Dad could hear her humming while she unpacked the groceries. He watched her out of the corner of his eye as she lovingly set the table for us.

He could hear the cheerful chirping sound of our voices in the distance as he approached the playground. He smiled picturing all of us in our favorite spots in this forest playground that was our little slice of heaven. JoJo and I had been talking all winter long about coming back to Beaver Brook. We were making plans, and chatting endlessly about what we would do when we returned to our forest.

By the sound of our chorus of voices, Dad knew we had reunited with our twin friends! He was glad they had returned! It made Dad's heart happy when he knew all of his kids were happy. And we were!

As Dad trudged along to call us for dinner, his foot hit something on the path. It was Duff, Connor's tired looking gray stuffed elephant and his constant companion. Dad thought Connor must be having a great time too, if he dropped his Duff. Dad reached down to pick it up and stuff it into his shirt pocket. He smiled at the rough treatment Duff must have been receiving from Connor since Duff was completely covered with dirt and pine needles.

Dad was thinking it was a darned good thing he found Duff because bedtime would be a nightmare without Duff easing Connor into sleep. He had recently given up his pacifier and it already would be hard enough to settle him down in the tent.

Dad spotted the tree house in the distance. Seeing the playground empty, he knew where we were. Dad imagined the kinds of tricks we must have conjured up to lure little Connor up that ladder. Mom would be beside herself if she found out we had climbed the ladder with him in our arms. She would think that was way too dangerous. He could hear her motherly tone scolding us, "Girls, what were you thinking," she would say.

Dad climbed the ladder in two quick giant steps and poked his head into the tree house. Seeing only the four of us girls inside, he asked, "Where's Connor?"

We all looked up at him in surprise. He exhaled, and his hand reached for the elephant in his pocket, that felt like a weight on his chest.

Chapter 11:

Mom kept glancing toward the forest path, waiting for Dad and us kids to come bounding out toward the table. She smiled to herself imagining Dad getting caught up in the moment. It was so like him to forget about dinner and, instead, dive into the obstacle course, competing with us like one of the kids.

Suddenly she remembered the burgers cooking on the open fire. She put an oven mitt on her hand and grabbed the hot handle, pulling the skillet off from the red-hot embers. As she held the skillet in her hand, she heard the urgency and fear in Dad's voice. The skillet made a thud as it hit the ground. "Connor, Connor, where are you buddy..." echoed through the trail.

Mom fled in the direction of his voice, with no thought of the steaming burgers lying on the ground.

Chapter 12:

The twins and JoJo startled and I gasped at the sight of my father in the doorway of the tree house. My blood ran cold and my heart quickened. Oh God, how much time *had* passed? I felt the color drain out of my face.

I started to answer, "I've only been a second...", but before the words were out of my mouth, Dad knew from the looks on all of our faces, we didn't know where Connor was. I had lost all track of time.

I looked down at my watch: 5:23. No, no, no, no. *Nine minutes.* It had been nine minutes!

Dad didn't wait for an answer. He immediately jumped down from the ladder, and began to call Connor's name. Duff fell out of his shirt pocket, and lay motionless in the dirt.

All of us scrambled out of the tree house and began to scatter to start searching for Connor. We could see Dad, hands pushing his hair back from his forehead, running his fingers through his hair as his eyes darted all around the play yard and into the thick brush. Dad started to holler Connor's name: "Buddy, hey Connor, hey little buddy, where are you little guy?" The longer he hollered, with no answer, the stranger his pleading voice began to sound. "Connor, let's go buddy. Dinnertime. Come on out," Dad called running back and forth and in and out of different openings in the woods.

"Let's go Connor. Mommy made you a treat! Mommy made you a sweet treat buddy."

JoJo picked up Duff and clutched it to her chest.

Ruby and little Rosie, the red headed twins, must have run back to their campsite, because before long, their parents joined all of us and were calling out Connor's name over and over again, "Connor, Connor, where are you? Come out little buddy."

I went over to the spot where I had left my little brother. Within seconds, weirdly, my teeth began to chatter. I guess fear can do that to you. Connor's little pile of dirt and needles sat at my feet. I squatted down, willing the pile to tell me where my little brother was.

My eyes swept back and forth and all around, looking into the woods, watching the adults beginning to swarm around, all calling his name. And then my gaze froze.

I saw Momma, near hysteria come out of the wooded path. Her look was desperate, directly at me. I started to run toward her, but then I stopped in my tracks. I knew what look she was giving me. It said, "You did this," without saying one word.

Mommy's face was white and her voice was tight and strained, "Connor, Connor baby. Connor you come out."

Her voice began to crack, "Come on Mommy's good boy. You come on out now. Come to Mommy's voice."

Each time she started to holler, the pitch of her voice sounded more agonized, "Little man. Come see Momma." She looked over at JoJo, clutching Duff to her chest. It seemed to inflame her panic to see that he didn't have his Duffy. "Come get Duffy Connor. Duffy needs you." It was then that tears began to fall.

Momma was clutching her cooking apron, grabbing the seams. She staggered around the play yard, peering into the shady woods, "Little buddy....little buddy..."

My heart fell further into my chest. That was the day I began counting to calm myself down. I have been counting to myself ever since.

I squeezed my eyes shut until it almost hurt, and began to count, "One, one thousand, two, one thousand, three, one thousand..."

I felt JoJo's hand on my shoulder and I reached for it. I kept counting all the while, holding fast to JoJo's cold, little fingers.

Not all storms have thunder and lightning.

Chapter 13:

The Beaver Brook Campground had a code for missing children: Kitten Alert. As it turns out, baby beavers are called "kittens". The owners of the campground, Mr. and Mrs. Theriault, held walkie talkies, and who knows who alerted them, but within seconds? minutes? they were there with their Motorolla walkie talkies in hand, trying to get Mom and Dad to remain calm. It was too late for that.

JoJo and I huddled together in a tight circle...holding one another...frightened to see our parents in such a panic. It had only been a minute, right? He was only two years old. How far away could he be? He would be right back. The twins' mother must have noticed us and stayed near as her husband joined the impromptu search party. Ruby and Rosie stayed close by with wide eyes and flushed freckled faces, tears forming puddles on the edges of their lashes.

Everyone searching had these competing thoughts running through their heads. I could hear them whispering, asking, shouting, hollering them to one another. What if he was in the woods? What if he had been taken? When was he last seen? What if he was near the water? And the last question: Why wasn't anyone watching him?

People were scattering in all directions, unorganized, and panic-stricken. "What was he wearing? When was the last time he was seen?" And of course, this question: "Who was with him?" Every time I heard that one, it was like a sucker punch to my stomach. Bald, fat, sweaty old Mr. Theriault, wearing his matching Beaver Brook baseball cap and sweatshirt, tried to bring some order to the group.

Those who were calm enough to listen, followed his orders. One person ran to the waterfront, another ran to alert others to help, another found a blueprint grid of the campground allowing Mr. Theriault a chance to map out orders for who would search each identified area.

Mom stood to the side of the forested play yard with wide horrified eyes, her fingers clutching and re-clutching one another, wringing her hands until her knuckles were pure white matching her even-whiter face. Her eyes kept willing one of the strangers to emerge from the woods with her little boy. Her Connor. I could see her mouth forming the word over and over again, silently, "Connor, Connor, Connor..."

I had to avert my eyes from my mother's face. I could not allow myself to see the pain. "One, one thousand, two, one thousand, three, one thousand...".

Behind us down the path, Camp Site, "lucky #7" was silent. Burgers lay in the needles. The red -checkered tablecloth held the meal that would never be eaten.

In the background, the name: *"Connor, Connor"* echoed deep into the woods, past stately tree trunks, through the branches, rustling the leaves, wafting off into infinity.

Chapter 14:

There are stories like this. You hear about children disappearing at campgrounds. Children, lost, who are never found. This story is not like that. Within minutes, a stranger, a huge hulk of a man from Camp Site #12, found Connor.

He spotted Connor's baseball cap. It was floating on top of the brook next to the play yard. Connor was found there.

It was that fast. The story has been retold and re-invented by all who were there, and by some who were not, but the common belief is this:

Connor quickly tired of playing with Duff, shortly after I left him to go to into the tree house. Most believe he was drawn into the woods by the sound of the babbling brook, or a bird, or a squirrel, and then noticed the beautiful running water...the stream running past with twigs and leaves and stones...enticing him closer, closer, ever closer.

He probably reached for one of those dappled shiny stones at the bottom of the running water. He was wearing little green crocs on his feet, the ones with the alligator eyes that he loved, and he most likely slipped on the stones, slick and smooth from the ever-running stream. Perhaps he bumped his head, when he fell, and lost consciousness.

His tiny baseball cap floated up next to him, a flag to the searchers saying: I am here. I am here.

Chapter 15:

Minutes into the search, a giant-of-a-man from Camp Site #12 wearing a bright yellow Beaver Brook t-shirt emerged from the woods, half running, half stumbling, hollering in desperation: "Help. Help me, help me," collapsing onto a pine needle bed in an opening on the play yard. In his arms he held a perfect blonde boy, a limp little form with one alligator croc on his foot.

There was a moment, when it seemed time was suspended. Everything stopped and was still. There was a single moment, when there was just a little boy laying on the ground, when my brother was found, and there was something like a feeling of relief. But it was just in that one second, and then there was chaos.

Connor was swarmed by medics and emergency personnel. They all rushed toward Connor's tiny body, as if lunging for the finish line in a race, equipment in hand. They went to work right away, hollering orders like a coach in a game. One shouted one thing, one responding, a question here, an answer back. Each playing a starring role in the fight for Connor's life. I felt like I was watching a movie.

JoJo and I held each other, watching, silent and breathless. The adult campers huddled around, looking toward the sky, whispering, hoping, praying the tiny body would come to life. Willing a happy ending.

Mom and Dad leaned over the medics, gripping each other, hollering Connor's name, pleading, grabbing the air, pulling at their own hair and clothing, begging a miracle.

As two men in white shirts still performed CPR, Connor was being moved to an ambulance that was backing up by the obstacle course. Mr. Theriault was waving his arms, directing them through his campground, keeping them from bumping into the spider web of ropes. Dad and Mom followed, turning toward JoJo and me, wordlessly knowing Ruby and little Rosie's mother would watch over us. JoJo and I watched our parents jump into the ambulance with our lifeless brother. The lights of the ambulance were an unwelcome and alarming intrusion on our wooded playground. Red lights spotlighting an angry, throbbing glare throughout the trees, the swings, and over the obstacle course like fiery fingers destroying everything.

In the background stood our tree house. It looked haunted to me now.

Chapter 16:

Everyone in the campground stood motionless, frozen.

My toes grazed back and forth against the little pine needle mound where Connor had been playing only moments ago.

The fire in Camp Site #7 was now orange coal. JoJo didn't even realize, until she looked down, that she was still clutching Duff in her tightly clenched fist.

Chapter 17:

JoJo and I were sitting on the wooden bench outside of Ruby and little Rosie's tent. Their mother, Mrs. B (I don't even know what "B" stands for) had placed a sign outside of their tent: "Home Sweet Home" with little birds around the edges, waving us inside. The cheerful birds made me nauseous.

Mrs. B tried to get us to eat something, but neither one of us could eat. It didn't look like Mr. and Mrs. B could eat either. Everyone was paralyzed, dazed, just waiting for some word about Connor.

As we were waiting, Mr. and Mrs. B would talk softly, shaking their heads, looks of worry lining their faces. Occasionally Mrs. B would walk over and brush the hair back on my forehead or Mr. B would offer a cold drink. Ruby and little Rosie motioned us over to their picnic table to color in a color by number book, and then, as the evening wore on to piece together a jigsaw puzzle of a forest scene, but it was hard for me to concentrate. JoJo searched out the edge pieces and I absently turned all of the pieces face up so we could see the emergent pictures. Eventually Mr. B lit a lantern and set it in the center of the table.

After what seemed like forever, in the distance, JoJo and I could hear a motor. Instinctively, we recognized the distinct motor sounds as that of our Daddy's Jeep driving toward us. The lights heading toward us through the woods ensured it was, in fact, our Dad. Mr. and Mrs. B, Ruby and little Rosie, JoJo and I all froze in the direction of the headlights moving toward the campsite. I dropped the puzzle piece from my hand.

I shut my eyes, and in my mind, "One, one thousand, two, one thousand..."

I heard the car door open with a creak, and saw Dad start to get out of the car. I wondered where my Mommy was. Dad hesitated a moment, and then rose to his feet. When he started toward us, I could hear him take a deep breath. He looked at all of us, huddled together, one to the other, and he tried to speak. JoJo and I broke away from the group and ran toward our father's arms, but the unthinkable happened.

Dad crumpled to the ground as we ran to him. His legs seemed to just fold beneath him. We had our answer.

Connor was gone.

JoJo and I held one another weeping, and then sobbing. We leaned over our crumpled father's figure, wracked with choking sobs. "Daddy, daddy," we both repeated over and over and over again waiting for his comfort.

I kept waiting for Daddy's arms to embrace me. "One, one thousand, two, one thousand, three..." They never came.

Eventually Mr. and Mrs. B stepped in to offer words of solace in a kind of chant, "Girls, it's okay, everything will be okay. Daddy is going to be okay. It's all going to be okay," the words were said over and over again. A rhythm of words, a song gently repeated, floating without any substance into the night air.

Dad gathered himself together, wiping his tears with the back of his shirtsleeve. Mindlessly he accepted the condolences of faceless strangers that stood around him, the flames of the campfire making the scene surreal, eerie, like a movie scene.

People asked what they could do. He had no answers. He explained that Rosie, his wife, my Mom, was sedated. She was in the hospital and he needed to get back to her.

He gathered up me and JoJo, "Come on girls," he said without inflection, backing away from the gathering and growing crowd. He thanked everyone weakly, his voice breaking again. We buckled up our seat belts in the back of the Jeep Cherokee, and we drove away, into the night, from Beaver Brook Campground for the last time.

Our tent remained behind, with its "WELCOME" mat outside of the screen porch and the proud pot of marigolds outside of the zippered door. Our air mattresses with the LLBean sleeping bags, all prepared and ready for us, were at Camp Site #7. The embers of the fire revealed the table, set and ready for a family that would never arrive.

JoJo and I both looked between us. There sat Connor's empty car seat.

On the drive away from Beaver Brook, the radio played, but no one heard the music. The three of us looked out from separate windows, into the blackness, lost in thought. All the way to the hospital, under my breath, I counted.

Chapter 18:

At the hospital, Mom's eyes were glazed and her face swollen from crying. Her head bobbed up and down with fitful sleep. She would jar herself awake, and moan softly, and close her eyes again.

JoJo held her face in her hands, tears squeezing out between her fingers, her tiny shoulders heaving with silent sobs. JoJo seemed to start to ask questions, but would stop herself before the words left her mouth.

I was frozen, paralyzed with the reality that I had been the one to leave Connor alone. I was choking on the guilt rising from my chest, as if two hands were squeezing my throat shut. If only I had another chance. I needed to have one more chance. I needed to count, "One, one thousand, two, one thousand, three, one thousand...please make it help...make it help, help it be better, four, one thousand, please, five, one thousand...."

Mom was discharged some time in the night, and Dad held her up as we walked silently in the dark parking lot toward our Jeep. JoJo and I held hands behind the shadowy figures of Mom and Dad.

As I counted silently in the back seat to somewhere in the thousands, I opened my eyes long enough to see Dad place his hand on top of Momma's hand. I startled as Momma jerked her hand away. Dad winced.

Clint Black started singing on the radio, *"Truer than true, you know I'll always be there for you..."*

For the first time JoJo and I could remember, Daddy didn't sing along.

The back of the Jeep that held all of our camping gear, so full of hope and plans, only 14 hours ago, was empty.

Daddy reached over and turned off the radio.

Chapter 19:

When someone dies suddenly, taken through an unthinkable tragedy, it's as if they have been removed from the earth by aliens. There and then gone. One moment in front of you, the next moment, vanished, evaporated, removed from the photo, deleted.

That's how it was with Connor. When we got home and somehow made it through the first night, from sheer exhaustion, we woke up to a house that included Connor. But he wasn't with us.

JoJo woke up first, and she climbed into bed with me. "Sissy, sissy," she whispered as her warm body snuggled next to mine, sliding underneath my pink comforter. "Is Connor in heaven with Grandma and Grandpa?"

I tried to answer her, but couldn't find the words. Even at eight years old, she seemed to understand and she snuggled in deeper.

"Sissy," Jo whispered after a long pause, "is it our fault? We shouldn't have left him."

"No, JoJo," I said firmly, "it isn't our fault. It's *my* fault. I'm the oldest. I shouldn't have left him."

It was then that little Jolene climbed out of my bed, went to hers and grabbed something. She padded back over to my bed and placed Duff into the crook of my neck. That elephant brought Connor into the room with me: his smell, his voice, his pudgy fingers. I reached up and took Duff into my own shaky hands, "It was my fault JoJo," I repeated.

JoJo didn't say anything else. I thought it must have felt good to her to have someone say it wasn't her fault. I kept waiting for someone to say that to me. I kept waiting for someone to say to me, "It is not your fault Lizzie." But no one did. Why should they? It *was* my fault.

I didn't know how I would be able to get up for breakfast that morning. I started counting but the noises downstairs kept interrupting. I wondered who had come to our house. We could hear voices, car doors, the sound of drawers opening and closing. What would be happening downstairs the day after your brother dies?

JoJo and I crept downstairs. We could hear the hushed grown up voices as we walked down the hallway. I could hear disconnected words and phrases, "...not your fault", "tragedy....", "....just a horrible accident," "don't blame yourselves...", "you can't believe it was your fault..."

The kitchen was filled with adults...some we knew and some we didn't. Neighbors filed in all morning. Dad, still wearing yesterday's camping clothes, hair ruffled, must never have gone to bed. He seemed to be answering questions, asking questions, trying to figure things out. When they spotted us, everyone froze in our direction and stopped talking.

Finally, our Sunday School teacher, Mrs. Torpey, came toward me and JoJo. She bent down, and smiled warmly, "Hey girls. Let me get you some breakfast." That was it. Nothing more. It was all that was needed to break the stony silence. Something normal. Breakfast.

While we followed Mrs. Torpey, the other grown-ups resumed their conversation. I recognized our minister, Reverend Torpey, as one of our visitors. We saw him in church, in a robe and in front of the altar. It seemed strange to have him in our kitchen, wearing faded jeans and a t-shirt.

JoJo asked, "Where's Momma?"

Mrs. Torpey looked down and said, "She is in bed resting girls. She needs some sleep. Let's just let her sleep for now, and you can see her later." We both nodded, and watched Mrs. Torpey crack some eggs into a bowl, one after the other.

In front of us, sitting on the table, was Connor's favorite book: *The Wheels on the Bus*. It was opened to the page where the bus driver says, "Move on back, move on back, move on back." Whenever anyone read this part to Connor it was always in a deep, deep voice. Connor would inevitably take his thumb and point it behind him, with a firm look on his face and a scowl, as if he was the bus driver.

Momma always said her girls were the chatterboxes and Connor "was a man of few words". But when we read *Wheels on the Bus* he would knit his brows together in a frown and say in his gravely voice, "Moo on back." It was his favorite part.

As Mrs. Torpey searched the cupboards for a pan, I looked around. The presence of Connor's absence was everywhere. His little sneakers, his Sponge Bob backpack, his sippy cups on the countertop, his bibs folded neatly in a basket.

Off and on, all day long, I kept counting, waiting for Mom's bedroom door to open, but Mom never got out of bed that day.

Chapter 20:

JoJo and I had stayed away from Mom's bedroom for a couple of days, so when she came out dressed for the funeral, we ran to her. Although we started to run with the intention of jumping into her arms, we immediately knew to stop ourselves in our tracks. She looked so fragile and unfamiliar somehow...thin and shaky, like a fawn just getting its legs for the first time.

My Mom is the most beautiful woman I know. Everyone probably thinks their own mother is pretty, but I know my Mom is because I hear it everywhere I go. People say to me, "Oh look at your dark hair and chocolate eyes. You are going to grow up a real beauty," and then they inevitably add, "Just like your Momma."

And, there's another piece of evidence that my Mom is gorgeous. One day Mommy was standing in the driveway watering her plants when Dad and me got into the Jeep. Daddy looked back at her in the rear view mirror as we headed off to soccer practice and said, "You know Lizzie, your Momma is special. She can just toss her hair in a ponytail and throw on a t-shirt and come out every bit as pretty as any of those Hollywood movie stars." Hearing that made me so proud. I kept thinking all day, "Like a Hollywood movie star."

Momma looked right through me and JoJo. She didn't say anything at all. Her hand was against the wall as she walked toward us, as if the wall was the only thing holding her upright. The day of the funeral was blistering hot, even for September, and already our hair was starting to frizz and wilt out of the tight buns Mrs. Torpey had formed out of our unruly hair.

JoJo and I wore matching navy blue dresses with white belts and open toed white sandals. Mrs. Torpey brought us to JCPenney's the day before the funeral. She came to the house, checked in on my parents, and asked if maybe we needed something to wear to the funeral. Dad just looked at Mrs. Torpey, not knowing the answer, and she took that for a yes. So she brought us out to the store, let me pick the look alike dresses and then she brought us out for lunch at Panera.

Ordinarily Momma would have said something about our dresses and our hair, but she just looked straight ahead, like a stranger, toward the door knob...like it was going to take all of her energy just to get to that door. We were invisible to her in that moment.

JoJo hated wearing dresses. I knew she felt trapped inside of her clothing. I chose the most un-fancy dress I could find, knowing she would be grumbly. She was a tomboy from the get-go, so without Mrs. Torpey knowing, she snuck her army shorts underneath her navy dress. On the way down the hallway, she flipped the back of her dress up for me to see she had shorts on. Even on this miserable, hot, depressing day...I laughed out loud. My laughter sounded so out of place.

Daddy was probably feeling as trapped as JoJo. He was wearing a navy blue suit and a gray and blue striped neck tie. He's a long haul truck driver, so the only uniform we ever see him wear is Levis blue jeans, t-shirts and his Red Sox baseball cap. He looked like a duck out of water.

He sounded pretty nervous telling Momma how beautiful she looked, "You look so pretty honey. You're doing great. We can do this. We're gonna be okay. Come on girls, come on," and Momma headed out the front door of our house. Daddy steadied her by holding her around the waist, and JoJo and I, holding hands, walked behind them.

Little did I know, I wouldn't see Momma walk out that door again for almost an entire year.

Chapter 21:

My sister and I go to Sunday school...most Sundays. Not all Sundays like some kids do, but we go pretty often. We're Methodist. Our church is a little white wooden church, like you see in paintings of the countryside, with a beautiful white steeple. We used to hold our fingers, woven together, and say this little saying: *"Here's the church, here's the steeple, open the door, and see all the people."* And then we would open our hands, and our fingers would be wiggling in the center of our palms like all of the parishioners in church.

That's what Connor's funeral was like. The church was full of people...like even more than on Easter or Christmas.

Reverend Torpey and his wife grabbed our family and had the four of us, Daddy, Mommy, me and JoJo walk in together, to the very front pew. JoJo and I clung to each other on our way down the aisle and Momma had to be held up by Daddy. She started crying so hard, I thought she was going to hyperventilate. Daddy looked afraid, and he kept whispering: "Shhhhh....honey, it's okay. It's okay." The noises Momma was making were like nothing I had heard before. They were barely human sounding.

JoJo and I just kept looking at all of the people. Everyone looked so upset and uncomfortable and they were reaching their hands out and patting us, and smiling sadly down at us. I even saw my teacher from last year, and my principal, Mr. Kelley. It was then that I thought, "Do they know I was supposed to be watching Connor? Do they know what I did?

Do they know I left him alone?" I held JoJo's hand so tight. That aisle felt like a million miles long with all of those people staring at me, and with Momma moaning and choking out sobs.

It was then that I saw where Connor was. In the front of the church was a tiny box. Connor must have been inside of that box. I grabbed the side of the pew and put my head into Daddy's sleeve, and started counting, "One, one thousand, two, one thousand, three, one thousand, four, one thousand...." I could smell flowers. The scent was too sweet.

I can't remember anything else about that day.

Chapter 22:

School starts right after Labor Day. This year, I was going into sixth grade. In my town, sixth graders go to Middle School, so JoJo and I would not be in the same school for the first time since she started school. That meant we had to ride on two different buses.

JoJo and I had been inseparable since "the accident". Daddy had been busy taking care of "details", whatever those were, and Mommy had been in bed. That left me and JoJo alone with only each other most of the time.

I tried to help JoJo get ready for her first day back to school. She was going to be a 4th grader. I knew Mommy would want her to wear something nice, but she gave me a fit. I gave up and let her wear jean shorts and a New England Patriots Tom Brady shirt. She wore red high top Converse sneakers and a ponytail on top of her head. Whatever.

Her bus came first and when she got on, she turned around and waved good-bye to me. "Have a great day, Sissy," I hollered, and for some reason I started shaking all over when I was left standing at the bus stop, alone. All the while I thought I was comforting her, but maybe she was the one comforting me.

When my bus came, I walked on slowly, keeping my head down the whole time. I sat at the first empty seat I came to, and didn't look left or right. No one said anything to me, and I didn't care. In my head, *I was counting.*

Everyone else had already started school, so I was starting Middle School already days behind. I had no idea where to go. The first day assemblies had been held the first day and all of the get-to-know you junk was over and done with.

It was a new school and it might as well have been a college campus to me. I didn't know my way around, and I was lost the minute I entered the building.

Luckily, by the grace of God, someone was already looking for me. A pretty, young blonde woman named Miss Fitz spotted me and grabbed me out of the hallway and into her office. It was kind of like those movies when you see people getting off the plane and someone is standing there waiting for them holding a sign with their last name written on it. She didn't have a sign, but she rescued me the same way.

"You must be Elizabeth Myers. I've been waiting for you," she said brightly. I was so relieved to have been pulled from the hall, I was horrified to find myself crying. Giant tears were streaming down my face. I just nodded, acknowledging that I was, in fact, Elizabeth.

"Hey now Elizabeth. I know you have been through a great deal. I am your school counselor, and I am here to make sure you get the support you need, and to make sure you find your way around this big place today," she smiled down at me handing me a tissue.

I pulled myself together and said meekly, "You can call me Lizzie. Everyone does."

"Well, Lizzie it is then," she said. "Why don't you settle down for a bit, and then you and I will tour this building together. I hope you don't mind, but I went ahead and found a friend for you to buddy up with today to make sure you feel comfortable." No sooner were the words out of her mouth, than in walked my best friend since kindergarten, Susan Fey.

I can't remember a better feeling than seeing Susan. I threw my arms around her and choked back salty tears. She was the familiar ground I had been looking for. Susan had been at my brother's funeral, but there were so many people there that day. She was at the funeral with her parents, and everyone was all dressed up and weird and awkward. We never really had a chance to talk or to be alone.

I don't know if it was me, or if it was her, or if it was that we were in Middle School now and not Fairfield Elementary, but Susan didn't seem like she was happy to see me. Her hug felt forced and cold. When I looked at her, there was a distance I had never seen before. She almost seemed embarrassed and frustrated to have to have me tagging along all day.

Did she know it was my fault that Connor died? Was that it?

Chapter 23:

I fumbled my way around the first day of school in a fog. Susan got me to each class and awkwardly said I could sit at her lunch table. A bunch of boys and girls I hadn't met were already sitting at the table, laughing and kidding around, until I arrived. Susan quickly introduced me to all of them, and the joking around immediately stopped. Awkward silence.

No one seemed to know what to say to me, so they didn't say anything. All of the joking and talking stopped and everyone just ate and exchanged looks with one another. Susan seemed like she wanted to die. Her arrival at the table with me spoiled all of the fun they had been having.

In fifth grade we learned about different idioms, like "the cat got your tongue" or "the straw that broke the camels back." I finally understood, in that moment, what it meant to "have an elephant in the room."

I wish they would have just kept right on talking and joking and laughing, and I wanted to tell them so, but I didn't know how.

I opened my lunch bag just because I didn't have anything else to do. There was the ham, cheese and mustard sandwich I had made this morning, wrapped in foil. I made one for me and one for JoJo. I imagined she was finding it just as unappealing as I was. I pulled out a tiny bag of goldfish crackers and ripped it open. I put one in my mouth. It sat there like cardboard. There wasn't one good thing about this lunch period.

Bit by bit, conversation re-started at my table. One girl was talking to Susan about her chipped nail polish. Susan grabbed hold of that conversation like it was the most interesting and important thing she had ever talked about.

I heard bits and pieces of what was being said, "...OPI nail polish never chips. It's the best kind. I never get anything else." Back and forth, the conversation traveled...moving onto shades of pink, blacks, glitter, and gel polish. Finally the sound of their voices was just white noise until the bell rang.

"Lizzie," Susan said with a note of irritation, "you okay?"

I jumped a little, coming out of my fog. "Oh, ya. I'm coming." I gathered up what I hadn't eaten of my lunch, tossed it back into the brown bag, and threw it into the garbage can being guarded by a blue uniformed custodian. We joined the herd heading out of the cafeteria, into the hallway. I blindly followed Susan, no longer feeling any comfort by her presence.

I met my teachers, one by one, as I entered each classroom. Of course, everyone else had already been there for days before me, so they all seemed "in the groove" but I was just trying to catch up and catch on.

Teachers were obviously trying to be extra kind to me; I could see that. No one came right out and said, "Oh Elizabeth Myers, the girl who killed her little brother. Welcome to class," but basically, I figured that was what the extra bright smiles and warmth was all about.

Quietly, before, after or during class, each teacher would sidle up to me and whisper, "Do the best you can," or, "Don't worry about this assignment," or, "If you need anything at all..."

Don't get me wrong. I appreciated the outreach, but really, what I wanted more than anything was to be anonymous. I wanted to be invisible. Dad and I are giant *Harry Potter* fans. More than once throughout the day, I was thinking: *If I just had that invisibility cloak.*

The last period of the day, Mrs. Reid, a petite blonde English teacher, of indistinguishable age, with wire-rimmed glasses followed me out the door. She wore a short floral skirt with a white blouse and a navy blue cardigan sweater. She had bare legs and flat navy shoes. She said my name, "Elizabeth," (Most of the time, I have people call me Lizzie, but somehow, I liked how my name sounded when she said it).

I turned around.

"Elizabeth," she said quietly and solemnly, but kindly, "this must be very difficult for you. You must have a lot on the back of your mind." I looked at her quickly and just nodded.

When I headed down the hall her words came back to me. *"You must have a lot on the BACK of your mind."* I whispered to myself, "I do have a lot on my mind, all right ...but it's on the FRONT of my mind, not the on the back of my mind."

And I went off, into the masses, to catch my bus. "One, one thousand, two, one thousand, three, one thousand, four..."

Chapter 24:

School comes easy to me. It always has for some reason. I can do my homework. I can keep up with my classes. I understand what I am being taught. I think I must be some sort of genius, but no one has discovered that yet. Seriously. I don't have to crack a book. I always get good grades, and really I am barely paying attention.

What isn't working for me is the friend thing. I can't crack the code. I can't figure out if it's me or them, but all of my friends from elementary school are staying clear. I don't really know why they stay away from me, but they do.

I mean, I never really was the type of person with a ton of friends. I really had one best friend, Susan. The other kids I was friendly with, but didn't have them over to my house or anything. I didn't think much about how many friends I did or didn't have, because there was always one friend by my side, and that was all I needed.

Susan and I grew up together. We went to the same nursery school, and then the same elementary school. We both were kind of quiet and we both liked school. We read the same books and we swapped when we were finished. We loved the *Junie B. Jones* series when we were in first and second grade. We read the *Little House on the Prairie* books when we were in third and fourth grade, and then we read all of the *Anne of Green Gables* books when we were in the fifth grade.

We loved all of the characters and would talk about them on the phone at night, draw them, make up our own chapters. When we played house, we were always on the prairie waiting for Pa to come home. We used to pretend we lived in a log cabin, with Ma in the kitchen baking bread while we would pretend to collect the eggs from our hens and we would make dolls out of cornhusks.

I miss having a best friend.

But Susan has a lot of new friends, and it doesn't look like there is a place for me.

Actually, it looks to me like everyone has friends except me. I walk to my classes alone and I walk away from my classes alone.

This is what my day looks like. I go through the following schedule:
Block 1: Science with Mr. Rodrigue
Block 2: Social Studies with Mr. Harris
Block 3: Math with Mrs. Dearden
Unified Arts with Mr. Barrows...this trimester it's woodworking...whatever...
Lunch: Disaster...sit alone...no friends...hate.
(This is when I count: One, one thousand, two, one thousand, three, one thousand, four...until that darned bell finally rings...torture)
Block 4: Spanish with Mrs. LaPorte
Block 5: English/ Language Arts with Mrs. Reid

The only tolerable block is block 5. It is there and only there that I feel a shred of hope.

And the good news, block 5 is at the end of day, so at least I get to end my days on a high note.

Chapter 25:

Block 5 was Mrs. Reid's class. Some teachers sit behind their desks madly organizing their stacks of papers before students come into the room. Some teachers run up the hall behind their students, making a mad dash for the classroom before the bell rings. Some teachers stand in the hallways gossiping with other teachers in between classes. Not Mrs. Reid.

Mrs. Reid always greets every one of her students by standing at the classroom door. When I walked into her room, it was kind of like stepping into a warm bathtub. I could feel myself starting to relax. Her classroom was calm, quiet and there was always some kind of quote or comment on the board that would make me think and wonder.

Every day there would be something like: *"Promise me you'll always remember: You're braver than you believe, and stronger than you seem, and smarter than you think."* A.A. Milne

Mrs. Reid may or may not be a kindred spirit. I am watching our relationship very closely.

She let us choose any book to read a week ago. I chose: *Anne of Green Gables*. I have already read that book three times, but she didn't say we couldn't read something we had already read. Anne has a best friend, Diana Barry. She and Anne call each other "kindred spirits." They are lifelong friends and they think just alike.

Mrs. Reid asked me to write a "Reader's Response Journal Entry." I wrote, "I used to have a kindred spirit. Her name was Susan. I thought we would always be kindred spirits like Anne and Diana, but I was wrong. I miss having a kindred spirit."

I was surprised at myself for writing so much. I really hadn't shared that much all year.

When I received my journal back, Mrs. Reid had written: "Elizabeth (I still hadn't straightened out the name thing), I think you and I might actually be kindred spirits. My favorite novel is Anne of Green Gables as well."

I must have read her words at least 100 times.

Chapter 26:

One afternoon, Mrs. Reid asked us to write something that happened when we were in grade school.

While I was brainstorming a list of different things that happened, I started to remember things.

When Grammy and Grampy died in the car accident, Mommy couldn't get out of bed. I was eight then, so I don't remember how long it lasted, but I remember sitting in her room, with JoJo.

We used to watch television on her bed. I remembered whenever we wanted to see Mommy, we had to go to her. She didn't really talk much then, so we would just sit on her bed and watch our shows. I would brush her hair or hold her hand. We just wanted to be near her.

I remembered how fragile she was...like a porcelain doll.

I kept trying to remember how long it took until she was herself again. Was it days? Weeks? Months? I want to remember so I can know how long Mommy is going to stay in her bed this time.

I did have one memory that stood out.

JoJo and I had been riding home from elementary school together on the school bus. Since Grammy and Grampy had died, we got off the bus all alone and went into the house to find Mommy in her bedroom, but on this day: our mother was at the bus stop! We were so excited. There she was. She was standing in her blue jeans and Converse high top sneakers, wearing a bright yellow Adidas sweatshirt, waving and happy to greet us.

JoJo and I could not believe our eyes! We ran off the bus and jumped into her arms. We were so glad to see her. She was smiling at us, either proud of us or herself or both, and when we walked into the house, our snack was waiting at the kitchen table....thick, warm banana bread slices slathered with chunky peanut butter and two glasses of ice cold milk with red and white striped straws.

That night, supper was hot and on the table when Daddy got home in his 18-wheeler. He walked in the door and immediately was greeted by the scent of hot buttered rolls, roasted chicken and rosemary potatoes and long spears of asparagus. He halted at the door dramatically, bent at his knees and took a long deep whiff of the hot dinner, and then swooped Mommy up in his arms and swung her around.

Mommy and Daddy both looked at us with a secret clearly being shared between the two of them. Mom nodded toward Daddy to go ahead and Daddy put his hand on Mommy's tummy. "Girls," Daddy said, "we are going to have a baby boy around here!"

Mommy was pregnant. The house was so happy. That night when Mommy tucked us in to bed, she read us the story: *Read to Your Bunny*. When she leaned over my bed, I said, "Mommy, I am glad you are happy again. I hated when you were so sad."

Mommy tucked my hair behind my ear and she rubbed her belly gently, "Honey," she whispered leaning toward me, "you never know what will give you hope." She kissed me goodnight and shut the door.

With the arrival of this memory, I realized, I had taken my mother's hope away.

Chapter 27:

At night, after JoJo and I were in bed, I would try to count myself to sleep. I guess a lot of people call that kind of counting, counting sheep: "One, one thousand, two, one thousand, three, one thousand..."

JoJo had her own room. Her room was right next to mine. Her room was always a major league disaster. Her bed was always unmade, a twisted chaotic assortment of sheets and blankets. I couldn't understand this because she always slept in my bed. Her clothes were stewn all over the floor, and toys were on every surface. If you didn't know any better, her room looked like it had been ransacked by a band of robbers.

My room was a different story. My room was immaculate. Mom and Dad always wondered how Jolene ended up being so messy and how I ended up being so neat. I couldn't stand having anything in my room out of place. My books were on the bookshelf. My clothes were hung neatly in my closet or folded carefully in my bureau. Top drawer for my underclothes, second drawer for my short- sleeved shirts, and third drawer for my long sleeved shirts. My bottom drawer was more crowded than I liked: pants on one side, shorts on the other. My closet was perfect. Dressy clothes hung on one side, casual on the other. My shoes were lined up in pairs on the floor beneath my clothes. On the top shelf, all of my sweaters and sweatshirts were neatly folded. Whenever Mommy's closet got messy, she would "hire" me to straighten it all out.

I loved straightening out my mother's closet. It smelled like her; everything smelled like vanilla and soft powder. I loved my mother's clothes. She didn't dress up very often, but sometimes she and my father had date night. On those nights, she wore dresses and heels and jewelry and make up. Other than that, she was mostly in soft, worn blue jeans with cotton sweaters or sweatshirts and Converse, colorful high top sneakers. One whole side of her closet was half zip jackets and yoga pants, all bright colors and matching. Lately, I never got asked to fix up her closet, because she was just in her terrycloth robe and pajama pants.

Every night, after I finished reading, JoJo would tiptoe into my room and snuggle up next to me. She had done it for so long, no one even mentioned it any more.

Since Connor died, JoJo always brought Duff with her. We never talked about it, but she just knew to tuck Duffy in between us. I would reach out in the middle of the night to make sure Duff was still there. He was our security blanket.

The nights were the worst. That was the time when my worries, that I had tried to contain all day, would rise up and get the best of me.

I worried that Mommy wasn't going to get out of bed. I worried that Daddy would get in an accident and not come home. I worried that I would forget to wake up and me and JoJo would be late for school. I worried that when I fell asleep I would dream about Connor. And my worst worry: I dreamed that Mommy and Daddy would never forgive me for what happened. And then I would begin to count: "One, one thousand, two, one thousand, three, one thousand..."

Sometimes, when I was trying to find sleep, I would hear Mommy and Daddy hollering at each other in their bedroom. BBB (Before Beaver Brook) Mommy and Daddy would sometimes "squabble" but they never would raise their voices. At least if they did, I never heard it.

Mom might be irritated if Dad wasn't helping with the dishes or laundry, or if Mom spent too much money on our school clothes...but nothing too serious. Mommy might say, "Jon, I'm not your maid. Come pick up your dirty laundry."

Dad might say, "If you want to be a stay-at-home-mother, you can't spend money like I'm an oil tycoon. If you keep spending money like that, you're gonna have to drive a truck of your own."

Those were the kinds of squabbles Mom and Dad had BBB (Before Beaver Brook).

ABB (After Beaver Brook) they yelled at each other a lot.

I would hear muffled words: "fault", "I told you not to let them go," "she was too young", "it was an accident, a horrible accident," "depressed," "you blame me", "I'm sad too," "bed," " you have to," "I can't do it all" and on and on and on.

A few times, JoJo would grab my hand while they fought. We never talked about it, but I knew JoJo was listening too. She pulled the covers up and tucked Duff in tightly between us, and we would both wait for the storm to end. Sometimes doors slammed, sometimes it sounded like something breaking.

I would pull my pillow over my head to muffle the words...but the words would drift through: "....they were too young," " he was too little...", "...why did you let him go...", ...I can't..." I squeezed my eyes shut.

I would count in my head, "Forty one, one thousand, forty two, one thousand..." I don't know what JoJo did to finally drift off to sleep.

One night after what sounded like a thunderstorm of words, I heard a door slam. I heard his truck start up. I ran to the window. Daddy left.

Chapter 28:

I drifted from class to class by myself. It was almost as if I had found Harry Potter's invisibility cloak, because no one at all seemed to notice me.

I got all of my homework done. I got good grades. I answered questions when asked. I didn't cause any trouble. Maybe I was invisible. I was invisible to everyone *except* Mrs. Reid.

All day long, I looked forward to the last block of the day. Mrs. Reid *saw* me. I could tell she really *saw* me, Elizabeth Ann Myers.

When I walked into the classroom, she would always make a point of saying, "Hello Miss Myers," and then, she would ask me a question or make a comment about my work. It was just a sentence or two, but it was the best part of my day.

On this particular day, ABB (After Beaver Brook), I could not wait to just see Mrs. Reid. As always, she was standing at the door, waiting with a smile. "Miss Myers, I really enjoyed reading your thoughts about the book *Wonder* last night. I read what you wrote more than once because it was one of the most thoughtful and insightful responses I have ever received."

I started to say something as a response, but instead, all of my angst...Connor's death, my guilt, my lack of friends, Mom staying in bed, and my Dad leaving... all rose up from deep inside to the surface. And I began, against all of my will, to cry, and count at the same time, "One, one thousand, two, one thousand..."

Chapter 29:

I remember once, after Grammy and Grampy died, Daddy held me and JoJo in his lap after dinner. We were rocking in the beige overstuffed recliner in the corner of the living room with my favorite slightly worn, cotton patchwork crazy quilt snuggled over the three of us. My Grammy had made that crazy quilt out of all of the leftover scraps of fabric she had in her house. She said all of the mismatched colors were what made it "crazy". To me, it was beautiful and worn out just enough to be super soft and cozy.

Mommy was pregnant with a big, swollen belly and happily humming and cleaning up the dinner dishes. Daddy kept peeking into the kitchen smiling at his wife, and all felt pretty close to perfect in our little world.

When he was rocking us, he said, "Remember girls, I told you Mommy was going to be all right. You know, when something bad happens, like Grammy and Grampy getting into that car accident, there are angels watching."

We looked up at him with big eyes like saucers and we gulped, "Really Daddy?"

Daddy nodded his head very slowly and with full conviction, "Oh yes, those angels are watching, and they form a plan to help us poor souls down here on earth."

We both were captivated by his words. "Like what Daddy. What sort of plan?"

"Well, when Mommy was very, very sad, those angels decided she would feel happy again if she had a little baby. The baby in Mommy's tummy is one of the angel's plans."

"Daddy, that was angels?" I said wide-eyed.

"Oh yes," Daddy confirmed. "Angels hold out their hands all along the way, and bring us back to safety."

We held onto every word Daddy was saying.

"When I was a little boy, we didn't have very much money. At one point, when I was your age, we didn't have one scrap of food in our refrigerator, and my parents told us they couldn't buy groceries for another week," Jolene and I couldn't imagine not having any food. We listened carefully to every word Daddy was saying. Daddy could weave a beautiful story.

"Me and my brothers and sisters were hungry as a pack of wolf cubs and we didn't have a dime in our pockets," Daddy told us shaking his head. "I went out for a bike ride, and when I got down by the bowling alley, I looked on the sidewalk and there was a $20 bill." JoJo and I looked at each other, both silently cheering for our Dad.

"I swear to this day, it was an angel's hand that dropped that $20 right in front of my bike," Daddy continued. "I went into the bowling alley, cause I didn't want to steal someone's money. I knew better than to take money that wasn't mine, even if I did need it."

"'No one has reported missing any money,' the man in the bowling alley said. 'Son, looks like it's yours.' To this day, I know it was an angel's hand, girls, an angel's hand that dropped that money right down on the sidewalk in front of me. That night my Mom and Dad went to the grocery store and got us bread, milk, bologna, cheese, butter, cereal, potatoes, beans and chicken. We ate like kings and queens." JoJo and I were left speechless when Daddy finished his story.

I think maybe Mrs. Reid has been sent to me by an angel.

Chapter 30:

Mrs. Reid seemed to know just exactly what to do when I started to cry. She knew I would be embarrassed to be in front of the other students, so she quickly ushered me into the hallway, and swiftly asked one of the sixth grader un-invisibles to have everyone begin writing in their journals.

I was trying really hard to get it together, but once the tears started, it was like a damn burst and I couldn't stop them. My face burned red with shame and embarrassment.

Mrs. Reid quietly led me by the arm, "Come with me Elizabeth."

I followed her without questioning where we were going. I think she took me into a teachers' lounge or something because there were half empty cardboard coffee cups with edges stained with lipstick, red pens and #2 pencils everywhere, and scattered run off papers and daily notices were strewn across the counter. A sign posted on the door said: *Clean up your own messes.* Apparently no one read the sign, or if they did read it, they ignored it.

Mrs. Reid scurried around trying to find a Kleenex on the cluttered counter top. Once she had one in hand, she pulled a chair up next to mine, and leaned toward me.

"Elizabeth, I've been waiting for you to come to me. I want to help."

I just looked at her blankly.

"What do you need dear girl? What can I do? I can see you are in a lot of pain."

That really was the million dollar question. I wasn't sure if I knew what anyone could do for me? What could help? I thought Mrs. Reid was great..the best...but could she turn back time? Could she wave a magic wand and stop me from going into that tree house? Could she bring Connor back to life? Could she get Mom out of bed? Could she conjur up a batch of friends for me? Could she bring Dad back home? Could she change my life for someone's perfect life with no mistakes in it?

Finally, I took a deep breath, feeling the weight and pressure inside of my chest pushing its way to the surface, and the words just came out, "It's my fault that my brother died. It was all my fault."

The words I had been keeping inside for weeks just sat there between us like a mushroom cloud.

There it was... the four million pound weight I had been carrying to every class with me, carrying on the bus with me, carrying home with me.

Mrs. Reid sighed and put her hand over mine, "Well Elizabeth," in a voice that was definitive and absolute, "that is simply not true. You are not responsible for the death of your brother," she said decisively, and there was absolutely no room for argument.

At that point, the tears could not be quelled. Mrs. Reid moved closer and I collapsed in a grown ups arms for the first time since Connor died.

Chapter 31:

When Daddy left, pretty much what was leftover of our lives completely fell apart.

He left us a note on the kitchen table that said:

Girls, I will be back but I need to leave for a couple of weeks. I have to take a long trip across the country for my work. Mommy needs this time to learn that she can do the things she used to do. I love you girls. Be good as you always are. I will be back. Everything will be all right. Daddy
P.S. Call Mrs. Torpey if you need anything.

I read the note out loud to JoJo and we looked at each other incredulously. At the end of the note, Daddy listed his cell phone number and Mrs. Torpey's number. "Is Mommy going to be able to take us places?" JoJo asked, tears puddled in her eyes.

I didn't know the answer. "I don't know Sissy."

I went into Mommy's room on the first morning with a glass of juice and a piece of cinnamon toast on a china saucer. As always, she rolled over with her hair tangled and her face lined with the imprint of her pillow. She weakly smiled at me. "Mommy," I told her. "Daddy left for a long trip."

"I know honey," Mommy said with no emotion. That was all she said.

"Are you going to get out of bed?" I asked fearing her answer.

"I am going to try, I am going to try," Mommy said with no further encouragement.

Every day, JoJo and I would come home from school, hopefully looking for one of two things...an 18- wheeler truck in our driveway, or our mother standing at the door. Neither happened.

What did happen was the food in the kitchen got lower and lower. I started trying to limit what we used, like we would drink ice water instead of milk. I would put one knife spread of peanut butter on the slice of toast instead of two. I would wash dishes with the bittiest amount of dish soap you can imagine. Eventually, however, the inevitable happened even though I was like a housewife rationing supplies in World War 2.

Those days I was counting more than ever. "One, one thousand, two, one thousand..."

The cupboards were bare. We started to run out of everything, like toilet paper and toothpaste and shampoo, and we weren't sure what to do. We hadn't been bringing cold lunch to school. We had been eating school breakfast and school lunch day after day.

We had a little gas station within walking distance of our house, and a couple of times JoJo and I went there and got one of their pale hotdogs and soggy buns out of the steamer. They also had some necessities like toilet paper and tiny tubes of toothpaste, probably for travelers who forgot things, but they didn't have full sized stuff for houses like ours.

Finally, one day, I told JoJo I was going to get Mommy to take us to the store. JoJo looked shocked. "You are Lizzie? How?"

"I am going to tell her she has to take us," I said bravely. "She just has no choice."

I walked into our mother's bedroom, and told her, "Mommy, you have to take us to the store. We don't have any more things we need."

Mommy rolled over and looked at me with the saddest look I have ever seen. She had dark, dark circles shadowing her eyes as if she hadn't slept at all, even though she had legitimately been in bed for the past few months. "I can't Lizzie." And she rolled back over softly beginning to cry.

"Mommy," I said, mustering up my courage one more time, my voice shrill with pleading, "You have to. We need things. We need food. We need toilet paper. We need milk. You have to take us. You have to get out of bed." And then in pure desperation my tone was stern, "You. Have. No. Choice."

Much to my complete and utter shock, Mommy sat up and slowly but surely got out of bed.

Chapter 32:

Mrs. Reid and I worked out a plan. (Or, maybe an angel had this plan worked out.) We had a journal that we kept between the two of us.

On the outside it looked like everyone else's Reader's Response Journal in a black and white notebook. But on the inside, it was just like we were Pen Pals.

Mrs. Reid told me to write down anything I was thinking....no matter what! She promised me she would write back to me every single day. And she kept her promises.

I tried it out on the first day.

Me:
Sorry about that crying fit in the hallway. You were really nice to me. I am embarrassed that I cried.

I tossed my notebook into the Reader's Response bin at the end of the period with everyone else's notebooks. I felt that twinge again... that spark of emotion...I believe it is called hope.

The next day Mrs. Reid started the period, as she always does, passing back the Reader's Response Journals. My face reddened when she passed me and winked ever so slightly as she handed my journal back to me, a sacred secret between us.

I tried not to appear overly anxious as I threw open my journal. There sat her script, letters perfectly formed in black ink.

Mrs. Reid:

You have nothing to be embarrassed about Elizabeth. Everyone has a breaking point! I cry too! I hope you listened to me when I said: You did not kill your brother. It was a horrible tragedy. It was a tragic accident.

Since I was in English class, I looked up the definition of tragedy. **Tragedy: an event causing great suffering, destruction, and distress, such as a serious accident or natural catastrophe.**

Me:
I looked up tragedy and it said it was a natural catastrophe. I was supposed to be watching him. I told my parents I would watch him and I left him alone.

Mrs. Reid:
That is called a mistake. You are only a young girl. We all make mistakes Elizabeth. You have to forgive yourself.

Me:
I don't know if I can forgive myself. I don't think my parents forgive me either.

Mrs. Reid:
Why do you say that Elizabeth? Why do you think your parents don't forgive you?

Me:
My Dad left us, and my mother can't get out of bed. She hasn't left our house since the funeral, and my Dad couldn't take it any more. He said if he left, maybe my mother would start doing the things she used to do. But she isn't. She can't. It's all because Connor died.

Mrs. Reid:

Your family has been through a horrible tragedy Elizabeth. Everyone is trying to deal with it the best that they can. Ms. Fitz, our guidance counselor, and I talked yesterday. I would like your permission to sign you up for a grief group. It is just beginning. There will be other students there who have experienced loss.

It could help you a lot. May I sign you up?

A group? Hmmmm...for kids like me, dealing with tragedies? I read and re-read Mrs. Reid's entry. I thought about all of my long and friendless, invisible days at school. Lonely walks in the hall, lonely lunches, lonely bus rides.

It was almost like kids were afraid they were going to "catch" my tragedy. They stayed away from me. Even my life long kindred spirit Susan didn't want to be around me any more. She looked at me like she almost wanted to talk to me, and then her group of "new friends" came along and would sweep her back up into her new crowd. Her new crowd of friends who didn't have the tragedy plague.

What if I got to meet kids that already were suffering from the "death disease"? That way, they wouldn't have to worry about becoming infected. They already caught it.

Me:
I think I could really use a group. Thank you. Sign me up.

Mrs. Reid:
Oh Elizabeth, you made my day! I signed you up. I think this group will do you a world of good. The group meets tomorrow in the guidance conference room during Unified Arts Block. I can't wait to hear about it.

Something felt different inside of me when I read Mrs. Reid's words: The group meets tomorrow in the guidance conference room…. I think maybe what I was feeling, was relief.

Since I was in English class, I looked up the word relief. **Relief: a feeling of reassurance following release from anxiety or distress.**

Yup, that was what I was feeling.

Chapter 33:

I could not believe my eyes when Mommy got out of bed. She and I locked eyes, and I just said, exhaling slowly, "Okay, then. Tell me when you are ready to go." It was weird to hear my own self, talking to my mother as if I was the grown up and she was the child.

JoJo was waiting for me outside of the door. As I emerged from Mom's bedroom , I gave her the "thumbs up" sign, and we high-fived each other. We were going to get some food into this house, and things were going to get back to normal.

I heard the shower running, and JoJo and I nervously waited as Mom took her time getting ready. I heard sounds coming from Mommy's room that I hadn't heard for a very long time. Drawers were opening and closing, the closet door creaked, a blow dryer was whistling its own happy tune.

After enough time passed, I gently knocked on Mom's door. I didn't hear a response. I slowly cracked opened the door and peeked through. My heart sank. Mommy was lying down again.

"Lizzie, I just can't do it," she sighed. Her hair was shiny and clean and she was wearing her favorite yoga capri pants with a shirt branding a purple peace sign. She had on her sneakers. She looked ready to go. We could not give up now.

"Mommy, you can. Come on. Please let me help you."

I grabbed Mommy's hand and started to pull her upwards. I could smell my favorite Bath and Body vanilla lotion on her. "You can do it Mommy. Please, you have to get up."

Eventually Mommy got up, but watching her walk to the door broke my heart. She winced, passing Connor's door, her fingers grazing the primary colored wooden letters affixed to the outside of his door that spelled out his name. The red C. The blue O. The green N. N. O. R. Her fingertips touched every single letter in a gentle caress. Her face registered her pain.

She kept her gaze fixed on the doorknob at the other end of the hall. I ran to get her car keys. JoJo ran to get Mommy's purse. This was going to be a team effort.

"Good job, Mommy. Good job," we cheered from the sidelines.

Mommy reached the doorknob on our front kitchen door, and clutched it in her hand. As she started to turn the knob...I could see her begin to shake. I quickly jumped to grab the doorknob for her, "I have it Mommy. I can get it for you," I said quickly, trying not to lose momentum.

I knew, maybe before she did, that she wasn't going to go out that door. Her knees began to buckle when I thrust open the front door. She braced her hands on the door jam, and stood there quaking. "I can't do it. I. Just. Can't. Do. It," she cried as she fell backwards away from the door.

JoJo reached her first, with Mommy's big purse over her little shoulder, and she gently said, "At least you tried Mommy. At least you tried your best."

Mom's voice was barely audible, "Lizzie, will you call Mrs. Torpey, from the church, and ask her if she will bring food over?"

I made my way to the telephone, counting to myself as I picked up the receiver. I dialed the phone, closing my eyes to the tears that were forming in the corners.

Mrs. Torpey promptly brought four bags of groceries into our kitchen that night. JoJo and I followed her around while she put them away. She had all of the essentials: apples, bananas, milk, eggs, bread, peanut butter, jelly, toilet paper, shampoo. She turned and asked us to find her different pots and pans as she pulled ingredients out of the bag. She placed a pan of fudgy looking brownies on the sideboard. She saw our greedy eyes looking toward the pan, and added, "Those are for *after* you eat your dinner girls."

Watching her put our groceries away made me think of Daddy's family when they went shopping after they found the $20 bill. Mrs. Torpey efficiently moved through our kitchen, putting things away neatly, each item exactly where it belonged. Every once in a while she would stop and clean up a stain, or more artfully arrange something on the counter. I felt embarrassed, as if I hadn't kept our home tidy enough.

Once all of the food was put away, she made a giant pot of spaghetti sauce, and boiled up a vat of noodles. She had JoJo and I set the table and she put a big, fresh salad and a jar of parmesan cheese in front of us. She poured us each a glass of ice cold milk, and had us hold hands and bow our heads in prayer, "Heavenly father, let us give thanks for the food we are about to receive. Amen." It was short and sweet, and then we dug in. We both slurped up two heaping helpings of the hot pasta.

When she finished cleaning up from supper and sprucing the place up, she turned and said she was going to go and visit with Mommy for a bit.

I didn't know if my mother wanted a visitor or not. I kind of figured not, but Mrs. Torpey didn't ask me. It was non-negotiable.

After a few minutes, I tip-toed and stood outside of my Mommy's bedroom. I wasn't sure if Mommy was up for company. What I heard surprised me, and I could feel my heart swell inside of my chest. I heard what sounded like praying.

I'm not sure why, but I got on my knees, bowed my head and joined them from the other side of the door. I could hear Mrs. Torpey's voice: "Trust in the lord with all your heart and lean not on your own understanding in all your ways, acknowledge him and he will direct your path. Amen." I whispered "Amen" too, and got up feeling lighter.

I heard quiet and steady talking, both Mrs. Torpey's and Mommy's voices. Back and forth there was chatting, and I heard muffled crying. After about an hour, Mrs. Torpey came out and fixed Mommy a cup of tea, brought it to her, and came back out to join me and Sissy.

"You girls have done such a nice job taking care of each other and taking care of this big house. Your mother is so proud of you, and I don't blame her. You are remarkable young ladies." JoJo and I beamed at the compliment.

"Would you girls mind joining hands with me, and saying a bedtime prayer before I head on my way?" We would never think of saying no to Mrs. Torpey. We both loved her gentle manner and calm, quiet way of teaching us in Sunday School.

88

JoJo and I stood at Mrs. Torpey's side in the hallway of our house. It felt weird, but good, to be praying outside of our church. We all held hands, and Mrs. Torpey began: "God, grant me great courage to wait with patience as you strengthen my heart. Amen." And then she gave our hands a little extra squeeze before letting go.

"Call me if you need anything else girls," she paused and looked at both of us very assuredly, "Everything is going to be okay. Healing hearts takes time." Then Mrs. Torpey bent down and gave each of us a kiss on the forehead.

Mrs. Torpey hesitated as she got to the door, her gaze moving down the hall toward Mommy's room. "Hey girls," she said too brightly, "how would you like to come and spend a few nights at my house? Just for a few days until Daddy gets home."

My stomach clenched and my face showed my worry. I couldn't leave my Mom, I couldn't. JoJo moved toward me, and we stood firmly together. "No thank you," I told Mrs. Torpey as politely as I could, but I am sure she heard my voice shaking. "We are just fine, and we need to stay here for Mommy." JoJo inched closer to me.

Mrs. Torpey's face registered our anxiety. "Well, how about this girls," she bent down closer to us, "I will pop by every day just to check on your Mom and to check on you."

We both visibly relaxed, and smiled at each other. "That would be great," I said, and I meant it.

As I watched her car back slowly out of our driveway, I said to JoJo, "Hey JoJo. Do you think Mrs. Torpey is part of the angel's plan?"

JoJo nodded as Mrs. Torpey's tail lights disappeared down our street.

Chapter 34:

The night was always the hardest.

I would count myself to sleep, but once I was asleep, I could not control my dreams.

Night after night, Connor would enter my dreams. It was then that I could hear his voice, "See me Sissy, see me." That was always what he said when he wanted to be picked up. "See me, see me," his arms raised in the air.

I would bend to pick him up, and the angry night Gods would interrupt.

I could never get my hands on him. I could never reach him. I would wake up and realize I was just dreaming...again.

I wanted my brother back. I wanted to 'see him'. I wanted to feel his weight in my arms. I wanted Connor back.

JoJo slept next to me. Maybe Connor made his way to her in her dreams too. I never knew. But many, many nights after I awakened from my dreams, I sobbed silently into my pillow, soaking my pillowcase.

One night, I fell into a fitful sleep. In my dream, I found myself back at Beaver Brook Campground. I could smell the fresh pine needles. I could see the tree house through the boughs. There at the end of the path, I could see Connor.

It was so good to see him. He was playing near the swings, holding Duffy in his hand. I could see the spoked B on his backwards cap. I started to run toward him.

"Connor, Connor, wait right there," I yelled through the trees. "Connor, it's me. Lizzie. Wait," and I ran and ran as fast as I could.

Connor started heading away from the swings, toddling in his little alligator crocs toward the woods.

I tried to catch up. He was so little, but I couldn't catch him.

Branches were hitting my face. "Connor," I screamed. "Connor, stop."

When I got to the swings, where Connor had been, I looked into the woods to find him. The woods were so thick. I didn't know which way to go. I chose a route.

Thick brush and thorny branches dug at my legs. Twigs for the pines slapped me in the face as I pushed through trying to find my baby brother.

"Connor buddy, Connor, answer me," I was crying now. "Connor, please, " and breathless I kept running. Where was he? How did he get away from me? I ran and ran.

Finally, I spotted a clearing straight ahead. There was a little patch where light shone through. I ran for the light. I broke through the forest, and there in the clearing stood Connor. He was reaching for a stone in the babbling brook in front of him.

I lunged in his direction, and grabbed him. He startled and turned to look at me. He gave me a big toothy smile, "Sissy," he said in his raspy two year old voice. "Sissy," and as he touched my face, I woke up.

Nooooooooo, no, no, no...

The nights were so cruel.

Chapter 35:

I was nervous all morning about going to my grief group. At the end of block 2, Miss Fitz, the young, pretty school counselor who met me on my first day of school came to collect me for our meeting. She walked quickly along next to me, the click, click, click of her kitten heels echoed in the empty hall.

Next to her, making my way down the hallway, I could hear her words of encouragement, "Lizzie, I am so pleased to hear you are joining our group. I think you will get a great deal out of it. I just wanted to be sure to grab you a little early to make sure you know it is a safe place for you. If you want to just sit and listen you may, but whenever you are ready to join in, you may do that as well. Whatever makes you feel the most comfortable." Her voice was so cheerful, and suddenly that seemed odd to me, considering the name of the group: grief group.

I had to move right along to keep up with Miss Fitz's fast pace, suddenly wondering what I had gotten myself into. Maybe it was just better to keep my invisibility cloak on. Being invisible wasn't all that bad.

Miss Fitz brought me into a conference room with about 10 chairs around a table. On the whiteboard, written in bold red letters were:
Group Rules:
- Every group member is valued.
- You have a right to pass.
- Listen with respect to those who are speaking.
- What is said in group, stays in group!
- Respect all rules of confidentiality.

That all sounded easy enough.

Miss Fitz had me choose my seat, and when the bell rang, one at a time, students started to file into the room.

I was surprised to see the boy who sat right next to me in social studies class walk in. Shortly after he arrived, a girl who was in my woodworking class came and sat right beside me. While others, kids I didn't recognize, continued to join our group, the girl next to me turned and met my eyes, "Hey."

"Hey," I returned.

"I recognize you from woodworking class," she said. "My name is Paula. I sit right past the table saw," she added with a gleam in her eye.

I liked her right away, "Hi Paula. I'm Lizzie."

Paula smiled at me, and said, "Well it looks like we are both part of the last group on earth anyone wants to be part of." We both laughed.

I have to admit. It felt pretty good, in that moment, to *not* be invisible.

Chapter 36:

Dad came back home. I got off the school bus one day in the late fall, and blinked twice to make sure I wasn't seeing things. Dad's giant big rig, his Kenworth 18- wheeler was parked in front of our house. I ran as fast as I could.

JoJo met me at the door. "Lizzie, Dad's home! Daddy came back!"

Daddy was standing there with a look I can't quite describe on his face: guilt maybe? But that expression didn't last long, because JoJo and I swarmed him with hugs and love! We were so relieved to see him.

Finally, when the reunion ended, we told him about Mommy trying to take us to the store. "Well I'll be danged, girls. That Mom of yours is one tough cookie."

I was shocked to hear Daddy say that. I thought he might be mad that Mrs. Torpey had to come and bring us food, but he wasn't. He sounded proud.

He quietly opened Mommy's door and we all went into her room with him.

"Hey there Rosie girl," he said, as he knelt next to her bed.

At the sound of Daddy's voice, she rolled over, and a tear rolled down her cheek, "You came back."

"I will always come back for you Miss Rosie," he said while wiping the tear away. "These little girls told me you were going to take them to the market," Dad said with a voice genuinely bursting with pride.

"I couldn't do it, Jon. I tried, I really tried, but I couldn't go out the door," Mom said with a mouth filled with defeat.

"Hey beautiful," Daddy said, "you tried. You tried. That's all that matters. I just needed you to come back to us. I didn't know what else to do, Rosie."

In that moment the unthinkable happened. Daddy started singing quietly in Mommy's ear: *"When I said that I do, I meant that I will...til the end of all time, be faithful and devoted to you...That's what I had in mind when I said I do..."*

JoJo and I slipped out of the room and gave Mommy and Daddy some time together.
We looked at each other and, in that moment, I know we both felt the hands of an angel on our shoulders.

Chapter 37:

Group began with Ms. Fitz reviewing the rules and then followed with each person in the room introducing or re-introducing him or herself. Ms. Fitz told us to first say our name, say our grade and tell what our loss was.

One by one, around the table, students said their names, and then they told their story of loss.

The boy in history class went first. "Hi," he said, looking down at his hands. He took a deep breath. "My name is Ross," another deep breath. "I'm in sixth grade." He slowly looked up, and glanced around the table. "This summer, my Dad died in a car accident." He looked at Ms. Fitz, not certain if he was finished or if he was supposed to say more.

Ms. Fitz quickly took the reins. "Ross, I am very sorry. Thank you for you willingness to share. I know it's hard no matter what, but it's especially hard to go first." Ms. Fitz nodded reassuringly at Ross, and then said to the next in line, "Okay, are you ready to go next?"

One by one, around the table, students said their names, and then they told their story of loss.

As it turned out, Paula, the girl in my woodshop class, lost her mother in the last school year. Her mother died of pancreatic cancer. All of these months later, Paula still could barely get her story out without tears. The wound still seemed fresh. When Paula finished, she croaked out, "I miss my mother Every. Single. Day." Her words hung in the room. We all nodded.

Students were there because they had lost a parent, a grandparent, because of a deceased aunt or uncle or special friend. One boy was there because his father was really sick, and he was going to die soon. He was in something called "hospice care." There were no limitations on the kind of loss you had to experience in order to be part of this support group.

Suddenly, Miss Fitz turned and faced me. "Lizzie, your turn. Would you like to share the reason you are here?"

I looked down at my hands, I almost started to count, but I stopped myself. "My name is Lizzie Myers," I said as clearly as I could. "I am here because my baby brother Connor died on Labor Day weekend," I had said it. I couldn't believe it. But there was more to be said, and I did. I took a deep breath, and added, "He drowned. He was only two years old."

It was out. Tears streamed down my face. Miss Fitz handed me a Kleenex, and Paula, next to me, put her hand over mine.

When I looked up, I saw all of the faces in the room looking at me. I thought their faces may be angry or disgusted: *There's the girl who let her brother die when she should have been watching.* No, it was none of that. What I saw was a room full of angels.

Before we left group, Ms. Fitz invited us to write a little note to the people we had lost. We were asked to think about something we would like to say to them.

"It can be anything. You can share a funny story, or something that happened that you wished they had been there for, or something really simple, like you miss eating ice cream with them," Ms. Fitz encouraged. She handed out little notecards with stars around the border and bright colored thin-tipped markers.

"Once you have written your note, place it in this wooden box, and you can head to your next class," Ms. Fitz pointed to a beautifully crafted wooden box that was painted light blue with silver glitter specks. Black letters were painted on the box, in calligraphy, that said simply, "What we wish we could say."

I stared down at my notecard, holding tightly to my purple marker. I closed my eyes, and there he was. As clear as day, I could see Connor standing in front of me, backwards baseball cap, saggy diaper, his sippy cup gripped in his teeth, holding Duff with his pudgy little fingers. It hurt to see him so clearly, and I didn't want to open my eyes, because he would be gone.

Slowly I opened my eyes. Everyone around me was writing. I could hear their pens moving along their notecards.

I began: I miss you Connor. I miss you every day. I should have been watching you. I would give anything to go back in time and watch you. I'm so sorry. I'm so, so sorry. I ruined everything.

I looked down at my notecard. And then quickly added: Me and JoJo are taking good care of Duffy for you.

I walked slowly to the blue sparkly box counting in my head, and dropped in my note to Connor. I didn't realize I had been gripping my note so tightly.

I saw Paula bring her note up to her mouth and watched her kiss the notecard before she dropped it in the box.

Ms. Fitz stood by the door. She quietly told each of us to take care, one by one as we filed, first past the box, and then toward the door. Before each student left, I saw her grab each student's hand and look into his or her eyes with a nod. Her face said, "You can do this," without saying a word.

And off we all went. On to the next class.

Chapter 38:

Mrs. Reid:
How was group Miss Elizabeth? I have been really curious to find out how you made out.

Me:
It was really great Mrs. Reid. I was surprised at how many kids were there. There were nine in the group, including me.

Mrs. Reid:
Oh, phew. I am really happy to hear you enjoyed it. You are one brave and strong girl Elizabeth. I admire you.

Wait. What? I had to read that line about 40 times. Mrs. Reid admires *me*? I couldn't believe my eyes!

Me:
Mrs. Reid, I am kind of embarrassed to ask, but why do you admire me?

Mrs. Reid:
I admire you because you have a quality called: resilience. You have shown the capacity to recover from a very painful and difficult situation. I admire that quality very much.

Well, who knew? I am resilient.

Chapter 39:

Ms. Fitz always started group right on time. We always began with a "quick check in". That's when we go around the table, say our names and how we are doing...just quickly, like: "My name is Lizzie and I am really missing my brother this week when I see the Halloween decorations. Connor loved Halloween," or something like that.

We always ended by placing a note in the blue, sparkly box.

One week, Ms. Fitz told us she was going to teach us some "strategies" for when we are having bad days.

She told us something I have really been thinking about a lot. She said we all spend 47% of our time not in the present. We spend almost *half* of our time thinking about the past or worrying about the future.

Ms. Fitz told us it is probably even worse for those of us who have lost someone.

I think she is right, but not about the future. I hardly ever think about the future.

I think, a lot, about the past. I think about when I went into the tree house. I think about when I left Connor alone. I think about what life was like BBB (Before Beaver Brook). I am stuck in the past.

Ms. Fitz taught us some "mindfulness" strategies. She taught us to take big deep breaths. When we breathe in, she says, "Blue skies in." When we breathe out, she says, "Gray skies out."

She said deep breathing helps us to clear our minds. It helps us focus.

She told us to listen to the sounds around us. When you hear the sounds all around you, you are in the present.

We practiced mindfulness every time we have group. "Blue skies in," deep, deep breath. "Gray skies out," exhale...

Mindfulness is a strategy, just like counting.

Chapter 40:

When Daddy came home, everything got a little bit better. It seemed like when he told Mommy he was proud of her, she started doing a few more things in the house. She seemed to push herself harder to spend time out of bed, out of her room.

In group, we learned about the stages of grief: denial, anger, bargaining, depression and acceptance. One night at the dinner table, I told Daddy what I was learning. He told me he thought he and Mommy were stuck in anger for a long time, and maybe now Mommy was stuck in depression.

"What's depression, Daddy?" JoJo asked, her spoon digging into her Shepherd's pie mashed potatoes.

"That's a great question Jo," he said. "Let me see if I can explain this to you in a way that makes sense." Daddy took a deep breath and put down his fork, "Girls, when Connor died, we all felt grief."

Our eyes were frozen on him, and I stopped chewing. Hearing those words made me instantly lose my appetite and my hands went ice cold. We had never ever talked, all together, about Connor dying. It jolted us to even hear the words, "when Connor died" even though we knew, all too well, that he had, in fact, died.

Daddy's forehead wrinkled and his face became very serious. He looked uncomfortable but he continued, "We all felt grief. We felt that deep, deep sorrow that Connor was gone." We nodded. "It's normal to feel grief when someone dies."

"Mommy is in a depression. She is feeling that deep, deep grief, but even though she stays in bed, she doesn't really sleep. She is having a hard time sleeping and eating and living a normal life," Daddy explained in a voice that sounded small and concerned.

"People who are depressed need help. Mommy needs help, not just from us, but from a doctor," Daddy added. "I was waiting to see if she just needed time, or maybe a push to do things on her own. But she needs more than that. I am working to get her the help that she needs."

Daddy saw the worry in our faces, "She is going to be okay, girls. Healing from depression takes time." He continued, "We will all feel grief from losing Connor our whole lives, but it will get better."

He seemed to be talking to no one when he added, "Time. We just need time."

He cleared his throat, and picked up his fork. He took a big bite of his dinner, and added, "Come on girls eat up," like he was showing us the way. We both hesitated, and then picked up our forks again. "It's going to all be okay. It's just a long road." The he added, "I'm a long haul truck driver girls. I know a long road when I see one."

We all ate in silence and then I had an idea. "Hey Daddy," I turned to him. "Maybe you and Mommy need a group like mine. Like my grief group." I looked up to see what he was thinking. "It's helping me Daddy."

Daddy looked at me and cocked his head to one side, "Now when did you get so smart, Miss Lizzie?"

I told you I was a genius, didn't I?

Chapter 41:

Grief group was on Mondays. It sounds weird but I looked forward to Mondays for just that reason.

That little conference room, with the ten chairs around the table, and the whiteboard with our posted rules, became my safe haven. I tried to get there early every week, so I would get to see all of my "friends" (yes, the "f" word), walk in the door.

I knew everyone's story.

Paula lost her mother to cancer. She always sat next to me.

Ross lost his father in a car accident. He would sit next to Jimmy at the end of the table. Ross didn't say much, but when he did speak, we all listened. One day he said, "Nothing is the same at home. Not one thing." I think we all understood that.

Jimmy, lost his grandmother. She had lived with his family for his entire life. Jimmy and his grandmother both loved Nascar. They used to watch the races together every Sunday.

Ben, whose step-brother died of a drug overdose, always wore his step-brother's school lacrosse jacket. It was blue and red and had our school mascot, the Eagle, on the sleeve. It had his brother's initials on the opposite sleeve.

Sara, who is an eighth grader, was supposed to have a baby sister. Her mother went to the hospital to have the baby, and came back with an empty car seat. Her baby sister died at birth. Sara said they still have the nursery all set up. This reminded me of how Connor's room is just the same as it was before he died. Sara hates going upstairs in her house, because she has to pass the nursery. Sometimes I feel like that too.

Joseph's father was killed last winter while serving in the United States Marine Corp. His father was killed by a car bomb in Afghanistan. He was a war hero. That didn't help Joseph's pain. Joseph always sealed his notes to his father with a purple heart.

Jasmine was an eighth grader with jet black hair and black lipstick. Her bangs were so long, you could barely see her eyes, and I always wondered how she could see us. She was in a terrible, fiery car crash that killed her aunt and her cousin. She was sitting in the back seat, so she survived, but she was haunted by that day, by her loss.

Barrett was always the last member of our group to arrive. He was always so funny and made everyone in the room laugh. He always had some wild story about why he was late. Last week he told us he was late because he had explosive diarrhea after eating the corndogs at school lunch. Even Ms. Fitz had to crack up about that one!

Barrett had dark hair and chocolate brown eyes. I always thought, even though his face had a smile, his eyes were sad.

Barrett's father was in hospice. He was diagnosed with ALS (Amyotrophic Lateral Sclerosis). Barrett's father hasn't been able to walk, or talk or chew or do any of the things he used to do. ALS destroys the people who have it, a little at a time. Ms. Fitz explained to all of us that even though Barrett's father was alive, Barrett has grief from losing his father *as he knew him.*

Barrett knew his father was going to die. He just didn't know when.

Chapter 42:

The cafeteria had green garland around the doorway, and the lunch ladies were all wearing red Santa hats with white pom-poms. I guess this was our school's attempt at being festive around the holidays.

I was still getting hot lunch at the cafeteria, because even though Mom was better, she still wasn't making bagged lunches for me and JoJo very often and I was sick of making them myself.

I was going through the lunch line, thanking the lunch lady for the chicken burger in a bun that she plopped onto my tray, when someone bumped into me, playfully, from behind.

I turned around and saw Paula, my friend from Grief Group. "Hey Lizzie, do you want to sit with me and Ross?" she asked.

I turned around and saw Ross standing behind Paula. He smiled at me and held up his fingers in a peace sign, "Yo, Lizzie".

"Yes," I said right away, and I meant it. Until they asked me to sit with them, I had no idea how much I wanted to sit with somebody.

Paula led me to "their table". Ross slid in next to us. Jimmy must have spotted us from across the room because he came over too. "Hey, hey, hey fellow Grief Groupers," he said as he swung a leg over the bench.

Everyone started preparing the food on their trays. I worked to open up my mayonnaise packet, Paula squirted some Ranch dressing on her chicken burger and Ross poked his straw through his chocolate milk.

Ross said to no one in particular and to everyone, "The holidays are gonna rot this year," with his mouth full.

We all nodded. Paula admitted that she didn't even think they would celebrate Christmas this year.

"My favorite holiday was Christmas and Mom would decorate every room in the house. She did all of the decorating. She bought and wrapped all the gifts. She stuffed all of the stockings. I don't know what we are going to do," her voice cracked, and then she added, "I don't feel like celebrating any way. Not without Mom."

We all understood. I hadn't even thought about Christmas this year, until I saw the decorations starting to sprout up around the school, a tree here, a wreath there, a string of lights around a bulletin board.

I surprised myself by adding to the conversation, "I don't think my Mom will decorate this year. We may not have Christmas either."

And there it was. The connection. My "me too" showed that Paula, I understood. That "me too", that's what makes two people kindred spirits.

Paula looked up at me and smiled. I started to put the mayonnaise on my chicken burger. Ross swiped a fry off my plate and dunked it in Jimmy's pool of ketchup. He crammed it in his mouth, and said, "Yup, it's gonna rot."

For the first time in the school year, I ate my whole lunch. The flavor of friendship made everything taste better.

Chapter 43:

Ms. Fitz knew Christmas was going to be hard on all of us.

As usual, I was the first to arrive at group. I was surprised to find a little, undecorated three-foot tree in the corner of the bleak conference room on a small stand. There were craft supplies on a tray in the center of the table. Ms. Fitz had put out paint and clay and tiny picture frames and fine tipped markers and plain white Christmas balls.

One by one, the group members arrived. Everyone looked puzzled by the arts and crafts. Paula sat next to me, as usual, her gaze taking in the materials on the tray, and then we looked at each other nervously and shrugged.

We started right on time. Ms. Fitz began by explaining to us that holidays are typically hard for families who have experienced loss. She told us that one of the problems is the "elephant in the room." Everyone knows why it's hard...because someone is missing...but no one talks about it.

"This week, we are going to create an ornament in memory of your loved one. I have prepared materials for you to use. You can sculpt, or draw or paint anything. The only rule is to create your ornament with your loved one in mind."

She began to pass the tray of materials around the table, and finished her instructions, "As always, you may pass if this isn't comfortable for you. Once you finish your ornament, you may take it home with you or leave it on the tree here. It is totally up to you."

I watched as my friends chose their supplies. They carefully began their projects. Each one, around the table, totally lost in their craft.

I decided to take a tiny frame and make a poem to place inside of the frame. I chose some fine tipped markers, a little piece of paper to write on and I chose a beautiful silver frame in the shape of a rectangle.

In my most careful handwriting, I wrote Connor's name down the side of the paper.

C: cutie pie
O: only 2
N: naughty sometimes
N: nice mostly
O: ours
R: remember always

At the bottom of the slip of paper, I drew a teeny tiny elephant and printed beneath it: Duff.

Looking at my ornament, I decided, in that moment, that I would put up our Christmas tree, even if Mom couldn't. I needed a place to hang my ornament.

When I got home, I helped JoJo make an ornament of her own. She painted a picture of Connor wearing his Red Sox cap on a red Christmas ball. She circled the picture with a line of Elmer's glue and sprinkled silver glitter on the string of glue. We placed it gingerly on top of an empty toilet paper tube so it would dry. It was perfect, and I told her so. JoJo looked at me, beaming with pride.

Chapter 44:

School vacation started on a Thursday. Wednesday afternoon ended with our entire school in the auditorium for a holiday chorus concert. We all filed into the auditorium seats and looked toward the stage. When the curtain opened, there were about 50 of our classmates, standing on risers. The boys all wore white shirts and black pants, and the girls all had on long black dresses.

The concert began by a very uptight little chorus director introducing the first selection: Jingle Bell Rock. She wore her graying hair in a bun on the back of her head. She had on a long black velvet gown with a red carnation pinned to her breast. She was tapping her sturdy black shoes to the beat of the piano, played by her accompanist on the side of the stage.

The chorus began singing right on cue, their voices bright and cheerful. Without warning, the music just got to me. *"Giddyup jingle horse, pick up your feet..."* I could feel the tears beginning in the back of my throat, pushing their way to the surface.

Oh no, oh no...I was thinking...not now...I can't cry now. Through the blurry tears, something on stage caught me off guard. Blinking to clear my eyes, I saw Barrett. He was in his crisp white dress shirt, in the back center row. He was singing at the top of his voice, his head thrown back, "...mix and mingle in a jingling beat...that's the jingle bell..."

I couldn't believe my eyes. Then it occurred to me. If Barrett, with his father home and dying, could be on stage, singing his lungs out, then I could get through this little holiday concert without crying.

Under my breath, I started to count, "One, one thousand, two, one thousand....". That helped calm me down. Then I would take a deep breath, "Blue skies in...."

I wiped the tears away from the corners of my eyes, and enjoyed the rest of the concert. I barely took my eyes off from Barrett. He sang like he didn't have a care in the world, snapping his fingers in time, swaying back in forth with the entire chorus. He was lost in his music.

But I knew the weight he was bearing as he stood on the top riser. I knew, as note after beautiful note came out of his mouth, he had EVERY care in the world.

Chapter 45:

When I got home, after the concert, Mom was in her rocking chair in the living room. JoJo was already home and on the couch watching Nickelodean on the t.v. with a bowl of Smartfood popcorn in her lap. "Mom," I said breathlessly, "it's almost Christmas. Can we put up the tree tonight?" JoJo looked up from the screen nervously anticipating the answer.

We both held our breath while we waited for her answer. Mom exhaled shakily and nodded at the same time. "We'll have Daddy pull it out of the basement tonight and you can put it up with him," she said in a voice heavy with emotion.

We did just that. When Daddy got home from work it was already late, but he saw the looks on our faces, and he went into the basement and yanked up our big artificial tree.

JoJo and I worked like two little carpenter ants untangling the lights without the complaint. Then we pulled the ornaments out of the old shoeboxes and threaded them with strings so we could hang them on the branches.

One by one, we held up the shiny decorations and admired them. Either "store bought" or homemade, they were a glittery, sparkly assortment. We pulled out ornaments made of pinecones, handprints, clothespins, and jingle bells. We pulled out spinning ballerinas and Disney princesses, souvenirs from family trips.

Finally, we pulled out a blue holiday ball with "Baby's 1st Christmas" written on it, and Connor's name and birthday written underneath. JoJo held it up nervously casting a glance toward Mom in her recliner. I could see that JoJo thought twice

118

about holding it in the air, and quickly attempted to shield it from Mom's stare. But Mommy had seen it.

Mommy slowly got out of her chair and walked over to the tree. She took the ball from between JoJo's fingers and held it in her hand like a delicate baby bird. She pressed it against her chest, and then to her cheek.

She went to place it on a branch, but could not release it. She brought it back to the chair with her and held it in her lap, rocking back and forth as we continued to decorate.

By bedtime, we had that tree up and decorated. When we were finished and Dad had given us his stamp of approval, JoJo and I went and got the ornaments we had made for Connor. We found a perfect special spot at the top of the tree, hanging them right beneath the angel.

Chapter 46:

One day, after holiday break, when I was walking to class, my best friend from elementary school joined me.

"Hey Lizzie," I heard the very familiar sound of Susan Fey's gentle voice next to me.

"Hey Susan," I answered cautiously. I wondered what she wanted.

"How are you doing?" she asked.

I didn't really know what to say. How am I doing? I mean, I was fine, but... that simple answer didn't really tell the whole story. But, I thought, "Well, my brother died, my mother is depressed and my life is kind of upside down," would not have worked, so I just said, "I'm fine."

Susan stopped me. "Lizzie," she said, her hand grabbing the arm of my sweater. "I am such a jerk."

I looked at her and I understood what she meant. My Junie B. Jones friend, my Little House on the Prairie friend, and my Anne of Green Gables friend, had really not been a friend at all when I needed her.

I didn't say anything. I just listened.

"I was trying to make new friends. I was trying to be popular. I was trying to fit in here. I am so stupid. I should have been by your side, Lizzie," her voice cracked. "I am so ashamed," she ended with a tear making its way down her cheek. "I should...," she continued but I couldn't hear anymore.

I found myself surprised when I started to cry, too. I am not sure exactly what I felt, but I began to cry with her. She was right. She should have been my side. I did need her. I needed her more than I have ever needed a friend, and my best friend wasn't there.

But I also forgave her immediately. "It's okay Susan," I said. "I forgive you." And I knew when the words came out of my mouth that I truly did.

I leaned in and gave Susan a hug. "I miss you Lizzie," Susan said to me. "I miss you a lot."

I laughed a little, uncomfortably, and said, "Well, did it work?"

She looked perplexed. "Did what work?"

"Did you become popular?"

"Not at all," she said. Down the hall came two familiar faces, both with big smiles, "But I see you are."

Just when she said that, Ross and Paula met me in the hallway. Ross linked his arm in my arm, "Ready for group?"

I looked at Ross and Paula, and I looked back at Susan. I pulled my arm out of his grasp and said, "I will catch up with you guys in a few minutes. I'll be right along."

I could see the relief on Susan's face when she realized I was staying with her. It was then that I told her all about my grief group and how it was helping me. I could tell she was listening to every word. She nodded her head and her eyes were filled with empathy and care. I found myself talking and talking and explaining about the group, until I realized I was going to be late.

Susan and I warmly hugged one another and I began heading down the hallway. I could feel her still watching me walk away, so I turned back around and waved, "Let's get together sometime soon Susan," I said, still moving backwards.

Susan nodded at me and shone a brilliant smile in my direction, "Definitely, let's" she said, and then added, " Hey you know, I still have those corn cob dolls we made when we read Little House on the Prairie."

I laughed out loud and said, "So do I," and she turned and left.

I left feeling the warmth of our friendship follow me all the way down the hall. And then I opened the door to group, and felt pulled into the glow of the room.

Chapter 47:

On Valentine's Day, our group decided to make wreaths out of hearts. On each heart, we wrote something we loved about the person we lost.

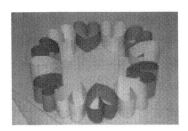

This activity was simple for me. I wrote lots of things about Connor. I loved the sound of his voice. I loved his giggle. I loved how he copied everything we said. I loved how he bobbed up and down when he heard the Mickey Mouse Club song, "Hot dog, hot dog, hot diggity dog…"

I was happy when I was cutting out the strips to make the hearts, and I wrote quickly with a red marker, listing the things I loved about my little brother. I got lost in my thoughts.

When Ms. Fitz interrupted us to share what we were writing, it jumped me. For a moment, I almost forgot the reason I was writing…because Connor was gone.

I listened as the other group members shared what they missed about their loved ones.

Paula missed the sound of her mother's voice when she first woke up in the morning. She used to pull down the covers of

Paula's bed to wake her up and she would sing: "Get out of bed, you sleepy head..." Paula said her mother did that every single day, until she got sick.

Ross told us he missed going ice fishing with his father. He told us as far back as he could remember, his father and his uncles and cousins would go ice fishing every weekend. They had an ice shack on Moosehead Lake, and as soon as the ice was ready, they would fish from sun up until sun down, grilling hot dogs in their shack and tossing sodas in the snow to keep them cold. They had snowmobiles they would ride on while they waited for their fish to hit. Ross smiled when he told about their ice fishing adventures.

When it was my turn to share, I stopped. A cloud must have come over my face, because Ms. Fitz held up her hand to quiet the others in the group, "Lizzie, are you all right? You look upset."

It was then that I shared. But I didn't share what everyone else was sharing.

"I, I..." I faltered.

"What is it Lizzie," Ms. Fitz urged.

"I just remembered," I began, "I remembered why I am doing this activity?"

Everyone looked puzzled.

"What, what do you mean," Paula asked, looking at me with concern.

"Well, all of you," I said looking around the table, "All of you lost people, but for me it's different."

"Lizzie," Ms. Fitz started, "everyone's loss is unique.."

I interrupted her, "But Ms. Fitz, Connor died because of me. Connor isn't here, and it's my fault," my face burned red with shame. My fists were clenched, and I said, almost in a whisper, "I was supposed to be watching him. It was my fault."

Chapter 48:

Ms. Fitz came around the table and put her hand on my shoulder. She told the group, "Friends, you can see our Lizzie here has a terrible burden she has been carrying around. First, let me say here, it was not your fault Lizzie. It was NOT your fault."

I couldn't hear that again. It WAS my fault. I was supposed to be watching him. It was my job. He WAS my only job. My heart was pounding in my ears. I was looking down at my clenched hands, and I could hear every beat of my pounding heart. As I started to count in my mind, I was interrupted by a voice.

"You were just a kid," said the voice. It was Barrett. "You still are a kid."

Once he spoke, everyone joined in. "Ya Lizzie", "it wasn't your fault Lizzie," "it was an accident"....I could hear the buzz of all of their voices at once.

"Lizzie," Ms. Fitz asked, "do you want to tell your story?"

I was shocked to find myself nodding. I wanted to tell my story. I wanted to tell my friends my story.

"Well, every year," I began, "my family and I always went to Beaver Brook Campground. We loved it there..."

I told the whole story that day. That day, I told them about the nine minutes I stopped watching my baby brother, Connor.

Chapter 49:

One day in February, when we arrived in group, Ms. Fitz began our session by explaining why Barrett was absent. "Friends, Barrett's father died last night." She paused, while we wrapped our heads around what had happened.

Even though we knew this was going to happen, it was still a shock. After a moment, she continued, "I wonder how you would feel about attending his father's funeral as a group? Naturally, this would be your choice."

I pictured Barrett. He was always making us laugh. Even though he was our group "class clown", he was still kind and gentle in his own way. I remembered that he was the first one who spoke up and told me Connor's death was not my fault.

One day, at the end of our session, he caught me off guard. We had both been standing at the painted wooden box, dropping in our letters, mine to Connor, his to his failing father, and he said, "I'm sorry about your little brother." I looked up, surprised at his words, and he said looking directly into my eyes, "He sounds like he was a pretty cool little dude."

I answered, "He was. Connor was really cool."

Ms. Fitz went on to explain, "Barrett was in a unique position. He was part of this grief group before he had actually, physically, lost his father. He bonded with each of you, and I thought maybe, we could all go to the funeral as a group to show him we care. No one understands what he needs right now more than all of you do."

I remembered the sea of people at my brother's funeral. I remembered how awkward and weird people were... no one knowing what to say.

Ms. Fitz looked at each of us, "So, what do you think about attending the funeral?"

I shocked myself by being the first to answer. "I'll go."

One by one, everyone in the room agreed to go to Barrett's father's service.

Chapter 50:

The day of the funeral there was a giant snowstorm. February in Maine generally is one constant, unending snow flurry, but this storm was a giant.

My father walked into my bedroom to make the announcement that school was cancelled. "Hey, hey, hey, sleep in today my beauties," he called out to me and JoJo. "No school today. It's a snow day."

I leapt out of bed, leaving JoJo in the toasty covers rubbing her sleepy eyes. "Oh no, Dad. The funeral is today," I blurted out instantly fighting back tears, running to the kitchen to look out the window.

It was just as Dad had said. There were already mountains of plowed snow, and more snow was coming at the window, blowing sideways. The television was on in the background with hundreds of school and business cancellations scrolling at the bottom of the screen.

"Lizzie, what funeral?" Dad asked surprised at my emotional reaction. Mom was sitting at the kitchen table stirring her tea, listening. I plunked myself down at the table and told Mom and Dad all about Barrett.

I told them how sick his father had been, how his father had died, and how all of the members of our group were supposed to go to the funeral together, as a team. I told them about Barrett making us laugh and being nice to me.

Dad looked at me like a stranger he was just meeting. "Dad, I need to be at the funeral."

I hardly ever cried, and when I did, Dad paid attention. Dad took a long look outside of the window, and he assessed the situation.

Mom looked up and firmly said to Dad, "Jon, she needs to be there."

"Well, you happen to be in luck young lady. Your father drives for a living," he told me. "I'll get you to that funeral Lizzie," he said, "and I'll go too."

I threw my arms around my father, "Dad thank you. We know how it feels, don't we?"

"We sure do little lady," Dad answered.

I turned to Mom at the table, and went over to give her a kiss on the cheek, "Thank you Mommy," she smiled weakly, and blinked back tears. I ran off to my bedroom.

I got dressed in my long beige sweater dress, and I pulled my boots up over my ribbed tights. I took the time to blow dry my long, glossy dark hair, pulled it back in a clip away from my face, and before I walked out of the bathroom, I put on just a little smudge of my Mom's lip gloss.

Mom walked us to the door. She took me by both shoulders and held me away from her at arm's length. "You look so pretty honey," she said through misty eyes.

I gave Mom a quick hug, and she whispered, "I'm so proud of you Lizzie. You are so strong." I walked out into the bitter storm feeling the warmth of my mother's acknowledgement and love.

On our way to the church, Dad picked up Paula. She was all bundled up in a long wool coat. With a gray knit scarf wrapped around her face so just her bright, blue eyes were peeking out. She pulled her scarf down below her mouth just low enough so she could whistle at me. "You look so pretty Lizzie," she said genuinely.

I told her, "I think you do too, but I can't really see you." We giggled nervously making our way slowly in the storm.

There were very few cars in the church parking lot. Mrs. Torpey was standing at the door when Paula, Dad and I walked in. She handed us a folded brochure with Barrett's father's picture on the front and written scriptures inside.

The sweet smell of the flowers hit me when I got through the entryway of the church.

The smell brought me right back to Connor's funeral. It must have done the same thing to Dad, because we both stopped short, and caught our breath. I slowly began to count while I gained my strength. The melting snow from our boots pooled around our feet, while we pulled ourselves together. After a moment, Dad grabbed my hand, gave it a squeeze, and moved me forward.

Country music was playing softly as we walked down the aisle to find our seats. I assumed Barrett's father must have liked that kind of music. Jimmy was already sitting in church with Ms. Fitz, toward the front, and he motioned for us to join. We scooted in beside them. Ms. Fitz smiled at all of us and we could tell she was grateful we had made the trip.

Barrett and his family sat together in the front pew. Several family members got up and spoke about Barrett's father. They made us laugh, so we could all see where Barrett got his sense of humor.

At one point, when something really funny was being told about a fishing trip escapade and a leak in a boat, Barrett turned around to look at the people behind him laughing. That's when he saw us.

I felt his eyes lock on me. I mouthed, "I'm sorry Barrett." He smiled warmly at me and turned back around to hear the rest of the story.

Chapter 51:

During school vacation, JoJo and I started having cabin fever! I mean, the snow was up to the windows and it was freezing outside...bone chilling cold. The kind of cold when you breathe in, your nostrils stick together...that kind of cold!

JoJo and I basically stayed in our pajamas all day. There was no reason to get dressed because no one was going outside anyway. I wore my flannel Pink pajamas with black leopard spots and fuzzy pink toe socks. JoJo wore her Joe Boxer flannel pajamas with army camouflage, and she tucked her pajama bottoms into her striped soccer socks that she pulled way up over her knees. We were the poster children of snow bound Maine children during school vacation. The lucky families flew out of Maine into warm weather in Florida, but not us.

The big news of the day was that Dad had ordered a new recliner for the living room. When it was delivered, by a snow-covered, freezing UPS man, it came in a giant Overstock cardboard box. There were little boxes inside of the big box, with all of the parts Dad needed for assembly.

Dad dumped all of the pieces out onto the floor and spread the directions out in front of him. He loved this stuff. He dove in like he was playing with a giant Lego set.

"Daddy," JoJo said, "Can me and Lizzie have the boxes to play with?"

Daddy didn't look up from the work in front of him. "Sure, honey," he said, "just make sure I didn't leave any of the pieces I need inside," and then he went back to the juicy job at hand. Mom wandered in from the kitchen.

"Hey babe," Dad said, happy to see her join all of us. "Want to give me a hand?"

Mom reached out to grab the directions Dad held up, and she nodded, "Sure. I can help you out," and she sat next to him on the floor, criss-crossing her legs spreading out the directions to read.

JoJo grabbed the giant box and begged me to play with her. "Lizzie, please play with me," she said, dragging the box that was taller than her, behind her.

Why not? I thought. I mean, I didn't have anything better to do. I had watched a million episodes of the *Gilmore Girls* from my boxed set, and JoJo and I had played *Apples to Apples* and *Connect Four* until we couldn't see straight.

We pulled all of the boxes over to the far corner of the living room and cleared out a space for ourselves. Once the box was sitting in front of us, JoJo blurted out her idea.

"Lizzie, this box will make a perfect tree house," she shouted out breathlessly. "It's just the right size. We can make it look just like the Beaver Brook tree house. We can put the door right here," she motioned with her hand, and then moved to the side, "and then the window boxes can go here..."

I held my breath.

JoJo must have seen the look of panic come across my face. She stopped mid-sentence and her face that had been filled with joy and excitement became red and angry.

My look immediately shifted over to Mom who had been sitting on the floor next to Dad. Mom slowly got up off the floor, and went quietly into her bedroom. Dad started to get up but then let her go.

JoJo stopped speaking mid-stream and ran into her bedroom and shut the door. Dad sighed heavily and started to get up.

"Dad," I said, "keep putting together your chair. I got JoJo," and I headed to her room.

JoJo's room gives me anxiety. She is a packrat and displays every single thing she collects. There is no shelf or surface that doesn't have an item on top of it and inside of it. She has shells and polished rocks and small figurines, and McDonald's happy meal toys everywhere. And God forbid any of us move any of these special items. She has a hissy fit! So I walked in and JoJo was sulking, head down resting on top of her knees, arms wrapped around her legs, sitting on the floor next to her unmade, tousled bed.

"Hey Sissy," I said. She didn't look up. "You didn't mean to upset Mom. It was a good idea to make a tree house out of that giant box."

JoJo sniffed back angry tears and wiped under her nose with the sleeve of her Joe Boxer pj's. JoJo hated to cry and crying just made her mad. "I just can't talk about anything Lizzie. I miss Beaver Brook Campground. I miss our other life. I miss our life before Beaver Brook," she paused and then added, "Our life before Connor died."

"I know JoJo." I sat down beside her. "I do too," and I meant every word.

"And I miss Connor," Jolene's shoulders started heaving up and down with her sobs. I put my arm around her and laid my head on top of her head. I could smell the soft floral scent of the conditioner she had used in her hair the night before.

"Me too Jo, me too," I said, tears beginning to form in the back of my throat, burning.

After a few tear-filled, quiet minutes, I had an idea.

"Hey Jo," I said, getting on my feet. "I have an idea. Go to my room, and I will be right there."

I went into the living room and got a box from the pile of empty recliner boxes still sitting in the living room. The box I grabbed was about the size of shoebox...all of the little tools and nuts and bolts had come packaged in that box.

I went around the house and collected markers and stickers and glue and tape and tossed them all into the box. When I got to my bedroom, neat and tidy and everything in its place, JoJo was sitting on my bed, waiting and wondering, with her eyebrows knit, showing her curiosity.

"Come down on the floor Jo," I motioned and plopped all of the supplies down in between us. "In group, we have a box called the "What I wish I could tell you" box. Let's make one for us to use at home."

Jolene leaned forward, interested, "What do we do with it?"

"Well, whenever you miss Connor, you put a note in your box. Or if you there is something you want to show him, or tell him, you put it in the box," I explained to her.

"Like what?" Jo asked earnestly, wanting to know more.

"Well last week at group, I made him a Valentine card. It had a Red Sox hat on the front and inside I wrote: I love you sport. And I signed my name."

JoJo and I spent the rest of the morning coloring and designing our box. We cut out pictures of toys and things he liked. We found all sorts of his favorite things in the pages of different magazines and toy fliers from the newspaper. We covered the box with pictures that we glued to the surface; pictures of cars and trucks and stuffed animals and balls and bats and Mickey Mouse and Disney characters.

When we finished, we agreed it was our masterpiece. JoJo brought it into her room and placed it in the center of all of her special collections. JoJo agonized over the first item she would place into the box.

Finally, she dropped a tiny seashell into the slot in the top with a note taped to it:
This is my favorite seashell. I wanted you to have it.
Love, JoJo

Chapter 52:

Bit by bit the snow disappeared and the harsh Maine winter surrendered into spring.

Mrs. Reid:
I've noticed a little more confidence in you lately Elizabeth. I wanted to mention it to you. You are standing a little taller lately. You are making eye contact more often. You may just be ready to take this school by storm.

Me:
What do you mean, "Take this school by storm?"

Mrs. Reid:
I mean you may be ready to show us just who you are Elizabeth Myers. When you started this school year, you had a great many shadows in your way. I think you may be ready for us to see your light. I hope you have a wonderful summer vacation Elizabeth. I have learned a great deal from you.

Me:
Thank you Mrs. Reid. I don't know what I would have done without you this year. Thank you for seeing me.

Mrs. Reid:
Elizabeth, I am not sure what I would have done without you this year.

Chapter 53:

In our last session of Grief Group for the school year, we found ourselves in the conference room, but the room was filled with drums and drumsticks. We all looked at each other, baffled. Drums?

Ms. Fitz predicted that we would be confused with the room filled with drums, so she began to explain right away.

"Hello my friends. Today we are going to learn a new strategy that research tells us is an effective tool for dealing with grief and trauma. We are going to learn about therapeutic drumming."

Ms. Fitz turned to the man next to her. He had long hair and a long beard and small wire framed glasses. He kind of reminded me of John Lennon from the Beatles. "This is my friend, Sean. He works with grief groups throughout the state of Maine, giving those grieving another tool to consider. Remember friends. What works for one may not work for another, but it's good to try all of these strategies to find what might work for you."

Sean quickly took over the group. He instructed each of us to place the drum between our thighs and he showed us how to hold the drumsticks. He lead us in some drills to get us started and bit by bit, the drumsticks started to feel more comfortable and natural in my hands. I looked around and watched my friends begin to get the hang of drumming. At first everyone felt awkward, but Sean made us all feel at ease.

Sean explained that those who chose drumming as a tool for healing seemed to heal faster. I could see how drumming would be an excellent distraction. When you were focusing on the beat and feeling the rhythm, you didn't have much room in your head for other thoughts.

Drill after drill, the drumming filled the room. It's hard to describe how good it felt to hit the drum, beat after beat. Boom, boom, boom dada boom, boom, dada, boom, boom.....hitting, hitting, boom, boom, dada, boom, boom. The noise filled the room. Sean lead us in beat after beat after beat....just follow Sean...just feel the rhythm, just listen to the drums...

Everyone in the room disappeared. All that was left was the sound. The beat. My heart. The drums. The drums.

And then tears. And drumming. And pain. And drumming. And regret. And drumming.

And missing Connor. And drumming. And wishing I had not stopped watching my baby brother for nine minutes. And drumming.

And when the drumming stopped, I took a long deep breath before looking up. Everyone in the room had tears streaming down their faces. We had drummed up the pain.

Chapter 54:

When I got home from the last day of my sixth grade year of school, there was a strange black car in the driveway.

I ran up the front steps and burst through the door to find my mother was showered, dressed and sitting in the living room with a man I hadn't met before. He was holding a yellow note pad, and he was writing ferociously as Mom was talking, looking at Mom over the glasses balanced on the bridge of his nose. Both of them looked up simultaneously registering my surprise.

"Lizzie, this is Dr. Ratner. He's working with me to help me get better." Dr. Ratner reached out his hand to shake mine. I took his warm hand without hesitation. If he was helping my Mom, he had to be one of the good guys.

"It's a pleasure to meet you, young lady. I have heard a lot about you this afternoon. You sound like a very capable and responsible girl."

His words left me in disbelief. How could he use the world "responsible" when describing me? Especially since he was clearly talking to Mom, and she *must* have told him how *irresponsible* I was when I was supposed to be watching Connor?

I looked at him suspiciously, and he must have known what I was thinking.

He started right in, "Lizzie, your mother told me what happened with your little brother Connor." My breath caught in mid-air. He did know.

Mommy interrupted when she saw my face go white.

It was in that moment that she said the words I had waited to hear for nine long months, "Lizzie, Connor drowned in a horrible, tragic accident," her voice started to quiver as she said these words, but when she said the next five words, her voice was strong: "It was not your fault."

Chapter 55:

It's funny how five words can change your entire life. 1. it, 2. was, 3. not, 4. your, 5. fault.

Don't get me wrong. I still have bad days. Sometimes, I have really sad days, especially around special occasions, like Connor's birthday or holidays. Those days are really hard.

In our grief group, we learned it's normal to have hard days . We try to make a plan on those days to do something different, so we aren't spending ALL day sad. Like on Easter this year, we went to the movies together, and then went and got ice cream instead of having an Easter egg hunt.

But knowing Mommy and Daddy didn't blame me for Connor's drowning at Beaver Brook helped me.

Mind you, I would give anything, ANYTHING, to have those few minutes back...the minutes when I climbed into the Beaver Brook Tree House and took my eyes off from Connor, but for some reason, life doesn't give us those kinds of second chances.

What I have learned in my grief group, is that we owe it to those who are taken from us to lead full and happy lives. Our group strongly believes that all of the people we have lost would not want us to spend the rest of our lives tangled up and twisted in grief.

So we go on. We move forward. And for me, I work hard every day trying to forgive myself.

After all, I am resilient.

Chapter 56:

One stifling, hot summer day, Mom, JoJo and I walked to the post office (yes, I did say MOM). I was stunned when Mom handed me a letter with the familiar handwriting of my beloved Mrs. Reid. I could hardly wait until I got home before I tore open the violet envelope with her delicate script.

Dear Elizabeth,

I have been thinking a lot about you lately. As it turns out, I really miss our "special journal". I am hoping next year, even if I don't have you in class, we can find a way to continue our communication.

I thought back to our ongoing "journal conversation" and it made me realize, we really are kindred spirits…like Anne and Diana in <u>Anne of Green Gables.</u>

You see, what I didn't share, was the fact that I lost my little brother when I was your age. He died in a house fire. His name was Daniel. I loved him very much.
I hope to hear from you Miss Elizabeth.

Most Sincerely in Kindred Spirit-hood,

Mrs. Reid

Chapter 57:

I sat with my letter for several minutes, trying to digest her words. Mrs. Reid truly understood my grief, my loss. She was my kindred spirit.

I immediately ran to my room to find the stationary I had received as a birthday gift from my mother. I knew exactly where it would be in my desk and I found the choicest sheet to write on, a beautiful cream pastel piece of paper as soft as cloth, rimmed with delicate forget-me-nots.

Dear Mrs. Reid,

I was so happy to get your letter. It's nice to have a kindred spirit in this world. I was so sorry to hear about your brother, Daniel.

I would like to tell you about my brother. I think you know his name was Connor. He always wore a baseball cap, backwards on his head....

Chapter 58:

Just before Labor Day Weekend, in the summer following my sixth grade year, there was a terrific thunderstorm in the forecast.

JoJo had been sleeping back in her room for the past few months, but, knowing a storm was on the way, we decided we would share a bed that particular night, so JoJo hunkered down in my bed for our thunderstorm sleepover. Over the summer, Mom had changed out my pink comforter for a "more teenage" looking comforter in stripes of green and lavender.

Come on JoJo, bring Duff...this storm is going to be s-s-s-scary!!

Sure enough, before midnight, the storm erupted outside of my bedroom window. We were prepared for anything...flashlights, water bottles, Pop Tarts and Duff!

Dad came in to peek at us one more time before he went to bed. Mom had gone to bed earlier. "You sure you two are okay," Dad said, teasing us. "You aren't too wimpy to handle the thunder?"

"Dad, go to bed. We're fine!" we told him, pushing him away from us.

Once he left the room and shut the door, I told JoJo, in my best big-sister- voice, "Now JoJo, I am going to teach you a strategy that I have used my WHOLE life when I get scared or worried and anxious." JoJo nodded in anticipation.

"What is it Lizzie?" she asked with Duff in a death grip.

"When you see the first bolt of lightning, you start counting, like this...one, one thousand, two, one thousand, three, one thousand, four, one thousand...until you hear the thunder. That's how you find out how far away the storm is. Lot's of people do it."

JoJo nodded. "Okay, let's try it."

Sure enough, within minutes a jagged streak of white lightning filled the sky and tore through the clouds, lighting up my lavender room. "Whoa....one, one thousand, two, one thousand, three, one thousand, four, one thousand, five, one thousand, six...." And then, a clap of thunder shook the foundation of our house as it stood. "Lizzie, that means the storm is six miles away!"

"You got it little sister. But I have a secret JoJo," JoJo looked up interested in what I had to share.

"What Lizzie?"

"In my grief group I learned that counting like this is a *strategy*. I use it whenever I get scared. If I have a big worry or I am really afraid...I count. It helps me."

JoJo nodded her head, taking the advice in stride, "That's a really good idea, Lizzie."

Storms don't always come in the form of thunder and lightning.

THE END

Tears, idle tears, I know not what they mean,
Tears from the depths of some devine despair
Rise in the heart, and
Gather to the eyes,
In looking on the happy
Autumn fields,
And thinking of days that
Are no more.

-Alfred Tennyson

I am so grateful for the loving support and encouragement of my husband, children, parents and my dear family and friends and colleagues who all read, and read, and re-read, and revised and revised and revised...and advised.

Your belief in me and in this project kept the wind in my sails and propelled me continually forward.

As you know, writing this book was a journey of healing. I know Lizzie's thorny path toward self-forgiveness all too well. I am almost there.

Oh, how I love you all...truly beyond measure.
Jenny

Made in the USA
Middletown, DE
04 October 2017